My Girlfriend is the Grim Reaper?!

Vol. 2

First edition

ISBN: 978-0-578-82365-2

Cover art by sateencat

To my wife, whose tireless patience and support throughout this project has helped see it become a reality. May it bring you even a fraction of the happiness you fill my life with every day.

girls' true nature, there wasn't (as much) to worry about while going out in public together.

At least, I hoped that'd be the case.

"By the way," I said as I pulled my arms through the frayed sleeves of the sweatshirt. "Have you seen Athena around? I was thinking we should try to get going soon – "

"You should know that I am always prepared, to the hour," Athena said as she made her way downstairs, clad in the jeans and long-sleeve shirt she'd grown so fond of since our museum outing. "I am perfectly ready to leave at any time of your choosing."

"Great, but why don't you put this on first," Lily stated plainly, holding out a large sweater. "You should bundle up like the rest of us."

Athena held up a hand and shook her head. "A true warrior faces the elements as they are. I need no extraneous garments to shield me from the chill bite of a nascent winter."

I took the sweater off of Lily's arm and held it up closer to Athena. "Be that as it may, a warrior should also be responsive to whatever the situation calls for." I shook the sweater in her direction. "After all, what would I do if my own mentor got sick?"

A faint blush rose in Athena's cheeks as she snatched the sweater from my hands, throwing it on in one swift motion. "If it is for your sake, then I suppose I've no choice but to oblige," she muttered.

I turned away, trying to suppress a laugh – at times like this she was somehow both much too easy and too difficult to understand.

Still, now that everyone was prepped to face the frigid night that awaited outside, I had a rare chance to see everyone dressed in more casual clothes – which, I had to admit, they all looked exceptionally cute in. Lily had on a purple knitted cap and dark grey jacket, while Athena was wearing a form-fitting white sweater and had her hair tied in a long braid (Lily and Nina had jumped at the opportunity to help her out with this earlier). Nina was sporting the plain, black sweater she had snatched from me, a frayed red scarf adding a splash of color to the otherwise dark blob of clothes she had become. I tried to insist that she wear a hat as well, but she was adamant that her ears would get in the way – a problem she did not appear to realize I was trying to deal with in the first place.

"Alright! Everybody ready to go?"

As we all gathered by the door, I checked my phone and saw it was 6:30 – still a little time until when we planned to meet Jun and Himeo, but getting an early start couldn't hurt.

"Yep!"

"Mhm!"

"Yes."

As I nodded and put a hand on the doorknob, I looked back to notice all three girls staring at me rather intently.

"Is...everything ok?"

Athena turned her head away and Lily looked down shyly, leaving just me and Nina staring at each other. She fidgeted in place for a moment before finally blurting out, "Master only has two hands!"

Even more confused, I cocked my head to the side, waiting for more of an explanation; however, none seemed to be forthcoming.

"Well, yeah, that's pretty typical of humans."

I felt Lily's cold touch as she took my hand in hers. "There's three of us, and only one of you," she said softly.

Finally, it all clicked – I hadn't given it much thought before, but – romantic implications aside – this was kind of like a date for all of them. After all, most of the people attending the Lunar Festival together were couples; no doubt all three had already figured that much out, and so might've developed certain...expectations for the night ahead.

I rubbed the back of my head awkwardly, unsure of how to resolve this present conflict. "I don't suppose you all could take turns?"

A momentary silence filled me with dread that I had already plunged us into a precariously awkward mood.

"Ok!"

"Seems fair~"

"I suppose there is no other way."

Maybe the moon's luck was shining on me, or maybe they had all grown closer than I'd given them credit for, but either way, after only a slight hesitation, all three girls assented without complaint.

Relieved to have avoided this potential powder keg for the time being, I took Lily's icy hand in my left, Athena's gentle, yet strong grip in my right, and followed behind Nina as she led us out the door and towards the outskirts of the town.

As we wandered this way and that, following a trail of faded lights that lined the sidewalk, I glanced up to see the moon full and luminescent, a soft orange set against the pitch black, dotted sky. I suppose you couldn't ask for a more appropriate night to celebrate a holiday like this.

Taking a deep breath, the slight sting of the last day of fall filled my lungs – it was a happy kind of hurt, full of nostalgia and hope for things to come. The past weeks might've been a rollercoaster of emotions and discovery, but in the end I found myself going to one of the most romantic events of the year hand-in-hand with two girls I'd found myself falling for more and more each day.

Two...girls...

I stopped in my tracks as a burgeoning realization resonated deep within.

Nina turned around when she didn't hear my footsteps behind her. "Master? Are you ok?" She looked at me with eyes full of care and concern, her left ear twitching curiously.

I snapped out of my momentary shock and quickly gathered my wits. "O-oh, yeah, I'm fine. Let's keep going." I forced what I hoped was a natural smile, which seemed to be reassurance enough, and she happily trotted forward, the rest of us continuing to follow behind.

It wasn't something I had given much thought before – what, if any, feelings I had for Athena beyond that of a student, friend, or caretaker. She was certainly...*unique* in her own way, but she had an undeniable charm that made me cherish each moment I was around her. Her self-seriousness could be intimidating, but it was tied to a natural wisdom and charisma that I found enthralling. The more I spent time with her, the more I learned about her past exploits and the stories she'd acquired, the more I felt myself drawn to her. I wouldn't hesitate to say I cared deeply for her, in a way so similar yet still so distinct to how I felt about Lily.

Still, there was no reason to think that – even *if* these feelings were romantic at all in nature, and despite any less-than-subtle displays of affection she'd shown – Athena had any interest in a relationship beyond what we currently had. Despite Lily's tacit approval of us sharing multiple partners, I still had no idea if that was the kind of thing I wanted in the first place, or how I would even make it work.

No, no – the best thing I could do is stay the course, and not be greedy with my own emotions. I had a wonderful girlfriend, a strict (but kind) teacher, and now – in addition to all that – an overly-attached and energetic housemate. That was more than enough, and so – at least for today – I would put those intrusive feelings aside and focus on just enjoying the night.

Speaking of which – it seemed as if even the festival itself was now reaching out to greet us. As we approached the outskirts of the city, an ever-more abundant series of paper lanterns snaked out along the sidewalk, flickering lights dancing this way and that in the gentle breeze. Each lantern was a different color, with a unique design painted around the sides. Some had been put up by local businesses, others as part of school projects, and still more just brought out by different locals who wanted to be a part of the festivities.

Nina carefully inspected each lantern we passed, darting her head back and forth to make sure she could see each and every one of them, while Lily only smiled contentedly, basking in the pale glow of the light. As I took my own time admiring the length of kaleidoscopic blaze beside us, I could just barely feel Athena tighten her grip on my hand. I gave a soft squeeze in return as, out of the corner of my eye, I caught the faintest glimpse of a smile fading from her lips.

A few minutes later and we at last spotted Jun and Himeo in the distance, with a third person standing just off to the side. I tried to wave them over, but found my right hand still very much occupied by Lily's. Regardless, it didn't take long for them to notice our fairly conspicuous group and run over to greet us.

"Hey hey, glad to see you all could make it," Jun said warmly, throwing his arms around me in a rough embrace, which I returned in kind.

"Yeah, well, it looks like not even death itself could stop me," I joked in a hushed tone. Jun rolled his eyes and punched my shoulder, as his attention quickly moved over to Nina.

"So, uh, you're adding even more girls to the harem now? I didn't take you to be that kinda guy."

"Gross." Nina was busy sizing up Himeo as her and Lily exchanged their own greetings. "Her name's Nina – me and Lily met her outside the arcade a week or two ago. Since she's from another world, too, she'll be staying with us for a little whi– "

I stopped short as I felt someone tugging at my sleeve.

"Master, what's a harem?" Nina was looking up at me with a face full of innocent curiosity, as much a source of danger as amusement.

"Oh, it's, uh…it's nothing." I tried to laugh it off and patted Nina's head, hoping she'd lose interest.

"That doesn't explain it at all!" She balled her fists and began hitting my chest softly.

Jun bent down and leaned over towards Nina. "You see, it's when a guy has lots of girls who love him, and they all mmph rmmph–"

"Annnd that's enough of that," I said, covering Jun's mouth and pulling him back up before he had a chance to corrupt her any further.

Nina tilted her head to the side, thinking it over, and then hopped in place. "Nina wants to be in master's harem! She loves master and, and she thinks lots of other girls would love master too, so that should make master happy!" She beamed up at me with unbridled pride, her earnestly simple logic difficult to argue with.

"Ah, that's very...nice of you to say, but I don't think that's the kind of thing you should going around telling the others," I mumbled.

"Ohh...so it'll be a secret between Nina and master?"

"Uh, right. So you can't tell anyone else, ok?"

"Ok, Nina will be good." She nodded sagely, placing a finger to her lips for emphasis.

"That's a good girl," I said with some relief, tussling her hair. I walked over to Himeo, now that the requisite excitement with Jun was out of the way, and gave her a pat on the back. "Happy that the festival's finally here?"

Himeo shrugged and shook her head. "There'll always be more work to do, just like last year." She paused and smiled faintly, nodding towards Lily, Nina, and Athena, who were all chatting together. "But seeing their reactions makes me feel like the effort doesn't go totally unappreciated." I could just barely overhear some of their conversation over the general din of the crowds nearby.

"And there'll be cakes and pies and ice cream, I'm sure," Lily said with a blissful smile, holding her hands to her cheeks.

"Woooooah! Really?" Nina's mouth was agape as she swiftly turned from Lily to Athena for confirmation.

"I've never been to a mortal celebration myself, but if it is anything akin to the like held in my own realm, I see little reason to doubt it."

"I heard Yuu say there're all kinds of games to play, too! Things like fishing and tossing rings and – "

"Nina can't wait anymore, let's go let's go!" She ran behind the two girls, trying to push them toward the tents and stalls that lay just ahead.

Seeing the three of them loosen up like this, I couldn't help but crack a smile. Up until this point it had just been one violent confrontation after another, but they now at last had a chance to relax and act like normal people. Or the closest thing to normal and people they all were.

As Nina continued her futile attempt to shove Lily and Athena forward, I took notice of the person standing two steps away from Jun again. "By the way – I don't think you've introduced me to your date over there."

Jun looked to his side and laughed. "Oh, yeah! Yuu, this is Mae. She's a first-year at our school, you might've seen her around before." She did look somewhat familiar, but I couldn't place my finger on exactly where. "And Mae, this is Yuu. He's been one of my closest friends since we were little."

"I've also been one of his *only* friends since childhood," I added, nudging Jun as I stepped forward. "It's nice to meet you."

Mae didn't say anything at first, only staring at me as if lost in another world entirely. Just as I was about to ask Jun if I had said something was wrong, she seemed to snap out of it and gave a brisk "Hello", bowing slightly.

Placing this rather stilted exchange aside for now, I took the chance to finally get a good look at Jun's date. She had short, brown hair, kind of like Nina's, and a round face with soft features. Her eyes were what I took most note of, though – they were an exceptionally dark brown, and although she seemed polite enough, I couldn't shake the feeling that there was something more to the way she had looked at me, like the vague recognition I had felt was somehow etched into her own retina. Still, I figured if she really did know me that well, she would've said something in the first place, so I kept these strange thoughts to myself.

"Masterrrr, let's go!" Nina had decided to change tactics and was now pulling me by the arm towards the festival grounds, as Lily and Athena appeared to have already started off ahead of us.

"Coming, coming," I said, nearly tripping over my feet as Nina continued to drag me along.

As we finally passed by the first stands, an overwhelming blend of sounds, sights, and smells overtook us. The air was filled with the scent of fried foods being served to customers left and right, the delighted squeals of children running around crashing with the distant hum of music from a band playing popular hits from a decade or so ago. All three of the girls appeared awestruck by what was before them – even Athena's normally calm and stoic presence was softened by a sense of childlike wonder and excitement.

"Ooh, what's this?" Lily asked, pointing towards one of the nearby food stalls. I took a closer look at the sign, trying to glean what was on their menu.

"It looks like…crepes, I think? They're these kind of light pastries with different fillings."

"Can we try them?" Her voice was full of boundless hope and expectation.

"Of course, of course. We can have anything you'd like."

"Master is the best!" Nina shouted suddenly from behind, jumping on my back. It took all my effort not to fall down from the weight of my unexpected passenger, but fortunately Athena was able to grab my shoulders and help keep me standing.

"Thanks for that," I said sheepishly, patting Nina's hands as she dropped back to her feet.

"Think nothing of it – children will be as children are," she said with a gentle smile, watching as Nina scampered off to go investigate some other set of vendors nearby.

Now absent the risk of being tackled from behind, I looked over the variety of flavors on offer and settled on an assortment – strawberry, banana, blueberry, and cinnamon. With requisite festival stall speed, I was handed my bounty after waiting only a minute or two, which I then distributed in turn to the girls. We all took turns trying each others' flavors, which Lily enjoyed to no end.

"Theshe are sho good!" she said through a mouth full of pastry.

"You should finish consuming your allotment before speaking," Athena reprimanded.

"Mm, you're just jealous you ate all yours already!" Nina chimed in, poking Athena's stomach.

In a surprising display of good humor, Athena laughed and shook her head. "I must admit it was quite the delicacy – I would not be opposed to another serving, though I'm sure there are many more such delights to yet partake in."

It seemed Nina really was too cute to get mad at, even for Athena – a power both impressive and disquieting in its implications.

We continued to browse the various food stands around us, picking up whatever treats caught our eyes. Lily still was drawn to anything with the slightest hint of sweetness, while Athena preferred more heartier fare, taking a particular shine to the several orders of meat dumplings we were able to grab. As for Nina…

"Master, master! Can we try this too?" As soon as we would finish up at one stand, she was already dashing over to the next, wanting to try near every new item she came across. I know she technically wasn't from this world, but I had to think that someone with such a small frame still had some kind of limit to their appetite.

"You...sure you're not full?" I asked hesitantly. "I don't want you to get sick."

Nina shook her head swiftly. "No, no! Nina's still hungry, food won't make her sick!" As she looked up at me with pleading eyes, I felt all my willpower melt away. Fortunately, I had been able to sock away some money here and there from my monthly allowance, so even Nina's seemingly bottomless stomach (or wherever this food was going) wouldn't prove to be too terrible a financial burden.

And so it was that at (long, long) last we made it past the nigh-endless array of food sellers and came upon the midway, where an equally abundant assortment of carnival game attendants waited to deprive us of whatever remaining money sat in our pockets. Jun briskly strolled over to the first game of chance he could find, a sort of modified roulette wheel with symbols rather than numbers, and started throwing down coins and calling out predictions as soon as he found an open spot.

"Is your friend taken to gambling by chance?" Athena asked with some concern.

"Nah, it just seems that for all the misfortunate he can bring to others, he's always been very lucky in his own, very unique way."

Sure enough, a few moments later a tinny bell began ringing as the attendant declared that they had a winner. After briefly scanning the shelves, Jun pointed to a small, stuffed bear, which he immediately handed to Mae. She smiled at the prize and hugged it tight, thanking him quietly.

"Alright, now let's see. Next up should be – " Jun turned

around with some surprise, as if he just remembered we were all standing right behind him. "Oh? You all don't have to wait around, I'm just gonna hang here for bit." With that he returned to the game, silently muttering to himself as he ran his eyes along the different sections of the wheel.

"You are…certain he is not taken by this vice?" Athena asked again.

"Uh, yeah. That's just Jun being Jun – let's let him have his fun for now."

I stepped away to head further into the fair when I heard Athena call me back hesitantly.

"I have…one more question."

"Hm? What's up?"

Athena pulled at the sleeve of her sweater, lips pursed as she struggled to bring what she wanted to say to the surface.

"Your friend just now, he…gave onto his date the prize he won." I continued to study Athena's face, trying to understand what she was getting at. "Is this type of ritual common among mortals?"

"I…guess you could say that. It's sort of a cheesy gesture, but it's not unusual for guys to want to win a prize for their dates when they go out like this. Maybe it stems from wanting to show they can provide, or just look good in front of them. Something like th– "

"I see," Athena said abruptly. "Thank you for sating my curiosity." She gave a curt nod to herself and began to stride away.

"Wait, wait, wait – wait," I said, grabbing the back of her sweater. "If you wanted me to win you something, all you had to do was ask."

Athena stood frozen in place, speaking in a hushed tone. "I…

do not recall asking you for anything such."

I sighed and let go of her back, shaking my head. "Then what if I just happened to give you a small gift while we're already here? Think of it as thanks for all you've done for me already. I may have a long way to go in my training, but you haven't given up on me yet. You'd let me do that much, right?"

"If you insist, then I suppose there is no hel– "

"Great, wait right there!" I shouted over my shoulder as I ran deeper into the midway, scanning the surrounding games for any prize she might like. Tucked away from the other stalls I spotted what looked like a decent choice – a row of plush turtles crowded a shelf, a dopey smile sewn onto each one.

As I approached the booth the attendant began to call out to no one in particular: "Another lucky contestant steps up to the plate, ready to throw his hat into the ring!" He flashed a toothy grin and placed three baseballs in front of me, the evident objective being to knock over the three bottles placed on a makeshift stool.

Of course, I knew it wasn't really that simple. With rare exception, each and every one of these games was sure to be rigged to some extent, though all that meant was you had to figure out the trick to winning.

As the attendant took a step to the side, I tried to focus in on the bottles' orientation, looking for anything that looked out of place or unusual. Given that the most obvious route was to just aim for the center, I was sure they had already fixed against that. I could aim for the base instead, but again, it felt too obvious to work.

"You gonna throw, or did you pay just to stand around admire my handiwork?" the attendant grumbled with a half-smile.

"Oh, uh, yeah," I murmured, picking up one of the balls and

eyeing the bottles. Athena's relentless training had certainly helped me get stronger, so maybe with enough force I could –

"Ooh, close, close! Try again," the attendant said as the first two bottles slipped off the pedestal, leaving the third standing perfectly straight.

After the bottles were set up again, I decided on a different approach – if strength alone couldn't win the day, then taking an unexpected angle (coupled with some copious luck) might be what I needed. I picked up the second ball and pulled my arm to my side, releasing it off my fingertips as I threw it at the bottom-left bottle.

As soon as the ball made contact, it ricocheted to the right, knocking the bottle next to it over and sending it spinning towards the edge. This helped knock the other two bottles away and, after few perilous moments of teetering, came crashing to the ground as well.

"We have a winner, we have a winner!" The attendant picked up one of the plush turtles and brought it over to me. "Congratulations young man, that's quite an arm you've got there." His lips turned up towards the shape of what I assumed was meant to be a smile as he spoke.

"Erm, thanks," I said with some embarrassment, hurriedly taking the prize and wandering my way back over to Athena, who towered like a monument in the middle of the packed street.

"Hey, sorry for the wait – I, uh, want you to have this." I held out the stuffed toy to her, which she reached for gingerly.

"Are you certain?" Her cheeks were flushed once again, her hand lingering over mine.

"Absolutely. I mean, I went ahead and won it for you, after all." I offered a reassuring smile as she still seemed unsure.

"Why..." she began. "Why this in particular, if I may ask?"

"It was cute – "

"Very we– "

"And it reminded me of you."

Athena took a step back, startled. "Y-y-you believe me cute?" she stammered, pulling the turtle close against her.

"No! I mean, well – yes, but – " I shook my head, trying to get back on track. "It reminded me of you because it's a turtle."

"A...turtle?"

"Mhm. I can tell you're slow to open up and quick to defend yourself, but you've shown just how much you're willing to protect the people you care about, too. And, uh, spirits and hybrids, for that matter." Athena carefully pulled the plush away from her chest as I continued. "I might be reading too much into it, but I have a feeling there's a lot more to you than what you've told me. And even if I'm slow to get there myself, I promise one day I'll get you to open up to me."

"You...would care that much?"

"Of course, you – "

"Yuu? Where'd you run off to?"

"Masterrr! Stop hidiiing!"

Lily and Nina's voices rose through the general din around us, bringing me back to reality.

"Shoot, I totally forgot we had wandered off from them. Sorry, let me just go tell them we're over here – "

"Hold." Athena gently grabbed my arm, her expression serious but kind. "Not one has told me the things you have said before. Though my gratitude is a small favor in return... thank you, nonetheless."

I flashed a quick smile and nodded. "Don't mention it."

As we worked our way through the throng of people and

met back up with the rest of our group, we found Lily sharing a plate of funnel cake with Nina (I suppose food was one of the things they could most bond over), while Himeo and Mae were likewise chatting a few steps away, and Jun continued to clear out all of the games of chance in his vicinity, a neat pile of prizes accumulating at his side.

"Mashterh!" Nina excitedly waved us over, still swiftly nibbling on funnel cake.

"Hey, there you are," Lily said, giving me an unexpectedly warm hug as I joined her side.

I returned the embrace and combed her hair with my fingers. "Yeah, sorry for disappearing on you like that all of a sudden. I forgot how busy things can get here."

"It's fine, it's fine – just don't go making a habit out of it," she said cheerily, burying her face against my chest. Normally I'd feel at least a little self-conscious about this much PDA, but I figured that tonight made a fine exception.

16

After engaging in a bit more exploration, game playing, and (at Nina's insistence) snacking, our group reconvened by the trickling ends of the festival stalls.

"The shrines aren't too far from here, so why don't we go check them out before it gets too late?" I offered.

Jun stretched and cracked his knuckles. "Yeah, I've just about gotten my fill of excitement, so I don't mind moving on." He was holding a bag filled to the brim with sweets and stuffed animals – alas, fortune ever smiled on him.

"It wouldn't be a bad idea to actually pay our respects, given that's the reason this festival even exists in the first place," Himeo added.

Lily tugged on my sleeve and whispered in my ear. "What's she talking about?"

I scratched my cheek, trying to recall what we had learned about in school so many years ago. "If I remember right...the Lunar Festival started many, many years ago, as a celebration to mark the end of the harvest season. I know a few related legends, but I'm not sure about the exact link to any of the shrines here, though."

Himeo clicked her tongue at me and shook her head in disappointment. "Our resident historian doesn't even know the story behind one of our most important cultural events? For shame."

"I can help explain," Mae chimed in suddenly. She had a soft, high-pitched voice, hesitant but rushed. "Farmers in this area used to believe that spirits would bless their harvest and give them good luck in the coming winter, when times were most difficult. The clerics that lived by built a bunch of shrines to honor these spirits, which were believed to be the closest link to where the spirits lived. So every Lunar Festival, when the moon was brightest and full, farmers would come seeking blessings of fortune and health." Mae gasped and covered her mouth. "Sorry, did I go on too long? I...I really like this stuff, and sometimes get carried away, and...nevermind."

Himeo nudged me and nodded towards Mae. "Seems you're in good company," she teased.

"Nah, nah, you're fine – I didn't know anything about that," Jun said in his usual good-natured tone, throwing an arm around Mae, who seemed to relax amidst this added reassurance.

"You probably *would* have known if you paid more attention in school," Himeo chided.

"I learn all I need to when I need to," Jun lazily retorted, with a sense of affection I felt only the three of us could detect. "Plus, I must be doing something right to make it to the top of the class."

Himeo laughed and threw up her arms in defeat. "You're impossible, but I'll give you that – you definitely know enough to get by."

"Hey, knowing how to work the system is just as useful as knowing how to work in the system," Jun replied with a smirk, eliciting a few giggles from the group as their back-and-forth continued a while longer.

"Alright, we can debate the efficacy of our current school system later," I said, rounding up my two friends and leading the others behind me. "For now let's actually get moving – we might even be able to get there before the place gets too crowded."

As we weaved our way through the crowds of festival-goers mulling about, buying trinkets and sweets and inspecting the various wares each seller was hawking, part of me couldn't help but relish the frenetic stream we were passing through. There was a quiet bliss to the solitude I once knew, but more and more I was coming to see what a hollow life that really was. Whether as a way to soothe my own ego or simply adapt to circumstance, I had grown to think that not only was isolating myself the preferred way to live – it was the *only* way.

Sure, I had two pretty close friends who I knew, on some level, genuinely cared for me, and even if I rarely saw my parents, they still supported me and reached out when they could. But who knew how long that would all last? People change, they move on. And I didn't intend to hold them back.

But maybe – just maybe – now I could find a way to keep going forward with them.

While I continued to mull over my changing relationships, we came upon the shrine's cracked stone steps. Compared to the raucous sounds of laughter and excitement just a small distance away, the pavilion was exceedingly quiet, with only the careful footsteps of a few other visitors to break the relative stillness.

"Master, what are we doing here?" Nina asked as we ventured towards the main plateau.

"People come here during the Lunar Festival to pray to the

spirits for things like good fortune, love, health – those kinds of things. It's a sort of local tradition."

Nina nodded firmly and balled her fists in determination. "Nina will pray really hard so her wish will come true!"

"Oh? What are you gonna wish for?"

She gasped, as if struck with an accusation. "Nina can't tell you master! Then her wish won't come true!"

I was pretty sure she was thinking of something different, but I didn't have the heart to correct her.

Advancing past the barren entrance, we arrived at a handful of plain, grey monoliths. Each one stood around 8 or 9 feet tall, with faint impressions mostly eroded away by a combination of the elements and time. A small, simple cottage sat at the end of the stone platform, where the shrine's keeper lived. Some volunteers came by regularly to help maintain the area, but the keeper himself was the one who attended to the actual shrines and any religious functions still carried out.

Each of us made our way to a different obelisk to pray, which served as a nice break to further reflect on the evening so far. Going out with all three of the girls was, predictably, more than a little hectic, but…I couldn't deny that I had really been enjoying myself so far. Despite the issues we'd faced (not least among them the regularity with which we were being attacked by monstrous creatures) and the fact that I was still mostly in the dark as to where they really came from or why they were here, I'd been finding happiness in even the smallest things we did together.

Kneeling down on the cool, uneven slate, I clasped my hands, closed my eyes, and tried to focus. So what was it that I really wanted? What was it that I could wish for?

Any other year I would have just thought of this as a trial in futility, a little diversion to engage with a local tradition and nothing more. Now that I'd met Lily and learned about the existence of spirits, however...well, it seemed like praying in a place like this might be something to take a bit more seriously than I first thought. Maybe that was why I had a hard time coming up with a specific wish? If this *was* somehow linked to spirits, and they really were listening, I wanted to make it count.

What matters most.

That question drifted to the front of my mind once again. I felt like it should be so easy to answer, yet here I was struggling to think of an answer.

Matters most.

Yes, I got it. I had pretty much drifted through life until this point, so I had never thought that hard about what was important to me.

Most.

It was at this point that I realized I was having an argument with myself over a random phrase I couldn't get out of my head. I tried to shake away whatever temporary insanity had overtaken me and focus back on the task at hand

I took a deep breath, closed my eyes once more, and tried to think.

Who, not what.

Goddammit. There was that voice again. Sighing in resignation, I said a quick prayer to at least have that question answered – to figure out what (or who, I guess) mattered most to me. However, as I opened my eyes, I was greeted with a rather unusual sight.

Lying at the base of the shrine was a small girl with long, lavender hair. Her skin was incredibly pale, almost translucent, and she was draped in a simple white and purple kimono with a floral design. My first thought was that she might be a relative of the groundskeeper, here to help out during the festival, but that didn't explain why she was now curled up in a ball in front of me.

"Hmph, I would not have guessed you would pray for such salacious things." Athena's stern voice snapped me out of my brief stupor.

"Master, is that girl your friend?" And Nina's.

"I-I guess it's ok, if that's what you like…" And Lily's.

I turned around and, to my mounting dread, found Jun, Himeo, and Mae also standing there as well.

"You know this isn't what it looks like, right?"

Jun walked over and propped an elbow on my head. "I dunno, with all these girls you've been collecting, who's to say you wouldn't wish for one more?" I swatted his arm away and stood up, flustered at the misunderstanding I was sinking further into.

"Even if these prayers came true – which they may or may not – how the hell would a girl materialize out of nowhere? And why would I wish for one?!"

Himeo snickered and tapped my cheek lightly. "You're always so easy to rile up. We know you had nothing to do with it – we just realized it was taking you a bit longer than everyone else, so we came to check on you, and found you with your eyes closed in front of this girl."

Upon hearing this my elbow jerked back, which, by unfortunate circumstance, just so happened to drive right into Jun's stomach. He flinched at the "accidental" blow, but quickly recovered.

"So, who is she anyway?" Jun asked as he straightened back

up.

"I really don't know. I knelt down, closed my eyes, and next thing I knew...well, here you go." I gestured towards the girl who, on a second look, appeared to be sleeping peacefully.

"Master," Nina said quietly, tapping me on the shoulder.

"Hm? What is it?"

"She's not a human."

"Alright, I'll – wait, really?"

Nina nodded, an unusually serious look on her face. We had already explained to Nina

how most people weren't aware of the existence of spirits and otherworldly creatures, so her rare discretion in these kinds of matters was appreciated.

I knelt back down in front of the girl and touched her shoulder, trying to wake her up. "Hey, are you ok? Do you live here?"

"Mm...cold..."

Given that she was lying down on the ground in near-winter weather with only what amounted to a thin layer of fabric to protect her, I had to imagine she was close to be freezing. Without a second thought I pulled off my sweatshirt and placed it over the girl, trying to wrap it around her thin body without disturbing her too much.

"Here you go, this should help a little."

"Mm...warm..."

I sat down and turned back towards the others. "What do you think? We can't just leave her by herself."

"Do you think she has some kind of family here?" Himeo asked.

"If she's really a spirit like Nina said, I doubt it," Lily answered, shaking her head.

"Ooh, ooh! Nina knows!" Nina was bouncing up and down, hand raised high in the air. "We can take her home with us!"

She beamed with pride as we all took a moment to process her suggestion.

"That's a sweet thought," I said, reaching out to ruffle her hair. "But we can't exactly go dragging a stranger home with us."

"You took Nina home though," she said, pouting.

"That's true, but you were also awake and agreed to it. We don't know what this girl's situation is."

She may be a spirit, like Nina pointed out, but I don't think we could just take her away without her consent.

"...bed."

The girl had started mumbling sleepily behind me, though I only caught the last word.

"Come again?"

"You...have...a bed?"

"Uh, yeah. Do you want to come spend the night with us? I hate to just leave you out in the cold like this."

"...really?" The girl's voice was exceptionally quiet and drawn, and it seemed like she had to muster all her energy just to talk.

"Uh, sure, it's no trouble at all."

I saw the faintest hint of a smile form on the girl's lips as I reached down to help her to her feet. When our hands touched, however, a warm, almost burning sensation returned to my chest. I tried to hide my wincing so as not to make it noticeable to Mae, though it still took me a few seconds to recover.

"A-alright, let's get going," I said as I tried to help the girl up to her feet, though she had already fallen fast asleep again, even while half-standing. With a lack of options available, I crouched down and shifted her to my back, throwing her arms around my neck and holding tight. "I'm sorry my hands might be a bit preoccupied on the way home," I told Nina awkwardly.

"M-master! W-would you really do something like that?" Nina said as she eyed me suspiciously.

Lily, ever my savior, came over and petted Nina gently. "He means he has to carry our new friend home, is all."

With apparent relief Nina nodded and threw her arms around my waist.

"That's ok then – Nina understands." She paused, glancing up at me. "And thank you master…No one deserves to be alone, not like this."

"Agreed." I leaned into Nina's hug as we all prepared to head home, yet another stranger in tow for the adventures unfolding before us.

17

"Hihi, we're home!" Nina shouted as we entered the house.

"Uh, Nina, you do know no one else is here, right?" I asked as I sidled past her.

"Well, yes, but the house might be lonely without us. So Nina makes sure to say goodbye every time she leaves and hello when she comes back!"

"Alright, fair enough – I'm sure the house is happy to see you too."

Nina giggled to herself and ran off, the bags in her hands rustling and jingling with each step. Jun had insisted that we take some of the prizes he won home with us, which I took as compensation for all the "jokes" he'd forced upon me earlier in the evening.

Despite her exceptionally light weight, my arms had gotten sore carrying our new friend on the long walk home, so I made my way over to the couch and laid her down. It looked like the bumpy trip here didn't rouse her in the slightest, as her eyes were still gently closed and breathing steady.

"What should we do now?" Lily asked, peering over from the other side of the couch.

"I'm not sure, honestly. She didn't make so much as a peep all the way here, and it seems like she'll be asleep for a while longer. I guess we just have to hope that she'll be rested enough in the morning that we can talk to her and figure out who she really is."

Lily nodded and moved next to me, resting her head on my shoulder.

"I'm glad you're the mortal you are..." she said quietly.

I turned to look at her, as she glanced in my direction. Her one visible eye was watching me intently, as if stripping away those prefabricated barriers between us and seeing to my core.

"What makes you say that?"

"Humans are scared of what they don't know. I mean..." She gave a bitter laugh. "Look at me. You're one of the few people to ever have been happy to see me."

I curled my arm around her head and combed her hair gently, feeling her absently tug on my sleeve in return. "I can't say I'm all that special, or that anyone else wouldn't have done the same thing if they were in my position." I paused, thinking through how I wanted to say this. "But still, even knowing what I'd be thrown into now, I'd always choose to do it all again, given the chance."

There was no need to say anything more. At that moment, the tightening grip Lily held on my arm said more in our hearts than all the words left in our breath.

"Mmph...bed..."

We were abruptly broken from this intimate moment by a small mumbling coming from the couch. We turned our attention back to the small girl lying there, but she remained completely still.

"She wants a real bed!" Nina popped out from behind the couch, startling the two of us and sending us stumbling to the floor.

As I hastily got to my feet and helped Lily back up, I tried to figure out what Nina was talking about. "A...bed?"

"Mhm! She says she wants to sleep in a real bed, that's why she came here."

Shrugging, I scooped the girl up in my arms and made my way towards the stairs. Her small frame and deep, rhythmic sighs only further emphasized how apparently vulnerable she was. I tried to not dwell on the idea of what might've happened if someone with worse intentions happened upon her first, and focused on the fact that at least Nina could serve as some kind of intermediary until she woke up.

"Hey, Nina." She was trailing close behind me as I went up to the second floor. "How did you even know what she was talking about in the first place?"

"Masterrr," Nina sighed, disappointed. "Nina already told you! She has super good senses, so she can hear things even you can't." She tapped the top of her ear for emphasis.

"Uh, right – still, thanks for helping me out like this." I couldn't exactly say I knew what she was talking about, but it was probably easier to just accept it for now and move on.

As we turned the corner and headed towards the end of the hallway, I carefully snuck one hand free from under the girl to open the door to one of our spare rooms. The bedroom itself was sparsely furnished due to its lack of occupants over the years, holding only a simple wooden bed, desk, and chair. Still, it should more than suffice for just one night.

"Here we are," I whispered as I lowered her to the bed. It wasn't the most luxurious of accommodations, but then again, I'm sure it beat sleeping on the ground.

I slowly covered the girl with some blankets and propped her head on a pillow, trying my best not to disturb her, though considering all she had been through and not stirred in the slightest, this might've been an unnecessary effort. I was about to walk away and leave her be when I saw a small frown form on her lips as she shivered under the covers.

"Huh? Are you cold?" I bent down to tuck the blankets in tighter, but Nina tapped my shoulder and shook her head.

"She says this isn't the right bed." I searched Nina's face for further explanation, but her expression remained enigmatic.

"The right bed?"

"Mhm, she wants to sleep with master."

In a night fraught with misunderstandings, what was one more innocent mistake?

"As nice a thought as that is, I really don't – "

I paused when the sleeping girl let out what I could only interpret as a happy mumble, her frown replaced by a small, contented smile.

"Is…that really what you want?" I asked carefully. She nodded ever so slightly, before returning to her near-comatose state.

Figuring this was hardly becoming an oddity at this point, I scooped the girl up again and carried her to my room.

"What's one more bedmate…" I murmured to myself as I laid her down and covered her tiny frame, trying to make sure she was as comfortable as could be.

I turned off the light to the room and began to close the door behind me when I heard the faintest of "Thank you"s drift through the remaining crack.

Smiling despite myself, I whispered back, "You're welcome," and left.

Once I finally made it back downstairs, I found the rest of the girls gathered together in the living room.

"How is she?" Lily asked, a tinge of concern in her voice.

"She's fine. I think. She still seemed passed out when I tucked her in, so we'll still have to wait until morning to find out anything more."

Nina popped up under my arm, grinning. "Nina helped too!"

I rustled her hair, to which she purred contentedly. "You did, you did."

Lily and Athena seemed curious, so I did my best to explain Nina's burgeoning "friendship" with our new roommate.

"I was never aware the power of hybrid beings extended so far…" Athena muttered to herself.

"Well, momma always did tell Nina she was special," Nina replied in earnest.

"Still, I'm worried about how little we know, like even just her name or where she came from," I said, resting my chin on my hands.

Lily turned to me with some disappointment. "You remember when you first met me, right? Spirits don't have names like mortals do, so I don't think you'll be able to ask her directly."

"But what about Athena–"

"I chose that of my own accord, once we were properly introduced. It seemed improper to not provide you with some means to address me."

I shook my head slowly, mulling everything over. While Athena had already suggested that the more spirits I contract with, the more otherworldly beings would find their way to me, it was starting to feel less like random chance and more like someone – or some*thing* – was helping to nudge things forward. The only question then was – to what end?

"Well, setting all that aside for now, I'm sure it's been a plenty fun and tiring night as is, so why don't we all try and get some rest ourselves?"

All of the girls agreed and, after getting changed into some proper nighttime attire, we climbed into bed, being careful not to move our fourth bedfellow too much as we tried to get comfortable. With little other choice, I laid the girl on top of my chest – I thought it might be difficult to breathe, but she was light enough that it almost felt like she wasn't there at all.

As I laid my head against the pillow, the entire night's exhaustion hit me at once, and I was quickly and blissfully able to fall right to sleep.

* * *

"Wake up, sleepyhead~"

I could faintly hear a voice coming from...somewhere nearby. It sounded unfamiliar.

"Wake up~"

I shook my head slightly, trying to will away whatever noise was trying to rouse me from my happy slumber.

"Really? C'mon."

Maybe it was just the delirium of being half-aware, but I felt sure that if I didn't respond, the owner of the voice would get the hint and leave me be.

"Fine, I tried~"

WHAM

"Huh? Who? What?"

With a jolt I shot up out of bed, a sharp pain lingering in my side. However, instead of encompassing darkness, my vision was overwhelmed by a piercingly bright white. I rubbed my eyes with one hand while I massaged my side with the other, trying to get my bearings.

"Are you finally awake? I swear, I thought you'd never get up at this rate."

As I blinked away the last of the excessive light and adjusted to my new surroundings, I was greeted by what appeared to be a familiar figure. A slight girl with light purple hair and shimmering violet eyes was bent over my shoulder, her face held less than an inch from mine.

"I kinda was trying to keep it that way…" I muttered as I planted my hands on the ground and brought myself to my feet. Looking down, I could see my initial assessment was correct – the next spirit to join our happy little family was standing right in front of me, donned in her flowery kimono and staring back up at me expectantly. Something still felt off though…

"Next time~," the girl said wistfully, "You should get up when a sweet maiden calls for you, so you don't get kicked." She winked and leaned forward. "Just a friendly word of advice from a world-weary traveler."

And, at last, it hit me (at least not in a literal sense this time).

"You're…awake?"

"Not quite." The girl smiled and shook her head in amusement, as if correcting a child. "Take a look around~" She stood on her toes and reached for my shoulders, pushing me to turn around.

Despite all I'd been through up until this point, I still feel I lack the words to properly describe what I saw. The simplest thing I might call it is a white void, but I could still feel there was something…more. There was certainly nothing at all around, and yet it didn't feel totally empty. A heavy presence seemed to emanate from all around, pressing down against my body and making my movements both slow and airy. There was plenty

I was missing, but one thing *was* for certain – this definitely wasn't my room.

"Anything look different?" the girl asked.

"Yeah, either there was an early winter blizzard and Lily forgot to close the window again, or this isn't my home..."

"Ehh, close enough for a mortal~" The girl stepped forward and grabbed my hand. "Here, sit down." She pointed toward what must be the ground, given that we were standing on it, though I was having no better luck in telling where one part of this place ended and another began.

Still, in some fear of receiving another swift kick, I did as I was instructed and stretched my legs out. Before I had a chance to ask what she wanted me to do this for, the girl threw herself on my lap, catching me off guard and knocking the wind out of me slightly.

Just as I was about to complain, she rested her head on my chest and closed her eyes. "You know...this is the only place I can do this."

"What do you mean? You still haven't even told me where we are. Come to think of it, you haven't even told me who *you* are."

The girl giggled and stretched her arms out. "I guess some explanations are in order." Leaning forward, she turned back to look me in the eyes, as if studying my features. "I'm sure you've already seen what happens when I try to talk in your world."

"You mean with the whole being asleep thing?"

She nodded slowly. "I normally only interact with humans here, in their dreams. So when I found myself in the mortal realm, well..." She looked to the side, smiling ruefully. "Suffice it to say I'm not used to it."

"So this is my dream?" I asked, looking around for anything besides whiteness. "Why is it so empty?"

"I dunno, it's your dreamscape. Maybe you just don't have that much of an imagination~" I glanced back down at the girl sitting on my lap, who blankly returned my stare.

A few moments later she cracked a smile, finally bursting into a fit of laughter.

"Ok ok, I've just always wanted to try saying that to a mortal at least once. Truth is, I wiped away whatever dreams you were having tonight so that I could finally talk to you properly, without any interruptions."

"I guess this *is* a bit easier than trying to talk through Nina exclusively. Although, since this is our first time talking like this, I suppose I should properly introduce myself. My name's Yuu."

I stuck out my free hand, as the other was busy holding the girl up, and which she awkwardly took herself, bending her arm close to her chest to grasp it gently. "It's very nice to finally meet you in person, er –" The girl paused and giggled. "You know what I mean. It's nice to meet you Yuu, I'm Luna."

"Luna…that's a really pretty name."

The girl's cheeks grew flush as she turned her face away. "Ever the charmer, aren't you? I guess I can see why so many of these girls have already fallen for you."

I was about to protest this unfounded claim when something occurred to me – she had told me her name.

"Wait, Luna."

"Hmm?" She turned attention back to me, having just as quickly regained her composure.

"How do you have a name?"

She tilted her head to the side, confused. "What do you mean?

Doesn't everyone?"

I tried to read her features for some kind of tell, but she remained as inscrutable as ever.

"Well, y'see when I met Lily and Athena –"

I was interrupted by a fast-familiar bout of laughter. "Sorry, sorry," Luna said, wiping a tear from her eye. "This is the first time I've had the chance to talk with a mortal in so long, I couldn't help myself."

I felt a smile forming, despite myself – I wanted to be annoyed at her feigned ignorance, but her innocent amusement was becoming infectious.

"Your friends are right – spirits like us aren't usually given names. Sometimes, however, humans will give us a name themselves, especially if we work close along aside them. Some of us adopt them, and some of us choose to remain nameless. Each one is different." She finished with a shrug and a smile, apparently neutral to the whole affair.

"So Luna comes from those old legends…?"

"Mhm! At least, presuming we're talking about the same thing."

I scratched my head, somewhat embarrassed. I tended to forget how near-infinite a spirit's existence could be compared to humans – what might seem ancient to us would feel like only a few years in the past for them, relatively speaking.

"It's just…I remember reading about some local legends from this area, and how you would be granted good luck if you prayed to the moon when it was shining the brightest."

Luna silently nodded along, waiting for me to continue.

"I…think the original legend went that a farmer hadn't been able to grow any crops all year, and was getting desperate. He knew that winter was fast approaching, and felt like he was out of options. So, feeling he had nothing left to do, he took a walk at night with the thought of throwing himself into the nearby lake. However, just as he was about to jump from a cliff, a soft voice called out to him. He followed the voice, and it took him to a clearing in the forest. The voice asked him to stay the night–"

"With the promise of a bountiful harvest for the next season," Luna finished.

I shared a half-smile with her and continued. "Unsure as to whether all that happened was a dream or not, the farmer decided put all his faith in the mysterious voice, and scraped his way through a difficult winter. However, come spring he continued to work the fields like he was told and, to his amazement, he was met with a mass of healthy crops just a few months later. When the other villagers asked about how he was able to grow so much, he told them the story of his chance encounter with a voice from the forest. The villagers decided to build a shrine where the farmer had stayed the night, and prayed to it for help in all sorts of things – often love, health, and wealth."

"I'm impressed," Luna said quietly. "I didn't think anyone cared about old stories like that anymore."

I paused, mulling the story and what she had said over in my mind. "That's kinda why we have that whole festival every year, and why we were there when we found you."

"Ah, so that's why!" Luna closed her eyes and nodded to herself, the forlorn tint to her voice having disappeared completely. "Mortals rarely visited that shrine anymore, so I was surprised when one came accompanied by spirits of all things."

"Wait, so that voice I was hearing – that was you?"

Luna giggled and began tilting her head back and forth. "Well, you see, normally I don't like to pry into humans' lives, but when something like that happens, and you haven't talked to anyone in so long, it's tempting to want to see what's going on, and so I thought maybe I could help you, since it has been a while since I assisted someone directly, and..."

I waved my hand in front of her, trying to dismiss the girl's worries. "It's fine, it's fine. Just – don't do it again, alright?"

"I make no promises."

Utterly defeated by this simple denial, I decided to take a different approach.

"Then do you mind if I ask something else?"

She smiled sweetly and leaned back, throwing one hand in the air. "Ask away!"

"What did you mean back there? About who or what matters most?"

An all-too-knowing look returned to her face as a devilish grin spread across her lips. "I guess that's just something for you to figure out, isn't it?"

"Wait wait wait, what about wanting to help directly and everything?"

Luna shook her head, her expression filled with pity. "What value is there in learning what matters most to you, if you don't figure it out for yourself?" She hopped off my lap and stretched out her back. "Besides, it's not like I can read minds. I only heard what was troubling you, and tried to get your thoughts in motion – the rest is up to you." She winked at me as she skipped away, the sleeves of her kimono fluttering in a breezeless wind.

"Wait, where are you going?" I tried to reach out, but my mind was growing hazy and my movements even more sluggish than before.

"I've kept you up long enough, so let's talk again some other night."

Her voice began to fade, distorting as it drifted past. And just as everything went black, I could hear one final remark.

"Goodnight, Yuu."

18

"Yuu..."

A faint voice called out to me.

"Yuu, wake–"

There it was again, with a slightly different tenor.

"Yuu, it's time to get up~"

The first voice returned. A vague sense of recognition washed over me, but I still couldn't bring myself to open my eyes. I hadn't slept this deeply in what felt like years, and I was loathe to have it end now.

"MASTERRRR!"

A high-pitched squeal accompanied the sudden proclamation as a weight came crashing down into my chest. I would've shot straight up if it wasn't for whatever had landed on me pinning me to the bed.

"Huh? Who? Why?"

Still in a daze, I struggled in vain against the creature pressed up against me, entangling myself in the sheets.

"Yuu, Yuu! It's fine, it's just Nina."

A chill overtook my body as Lily placed a hand on my shoulder, her brow furrowed with concern. While my senses slowly returned, I could finally see that, just as she said, Nina was straddling my chest and staring at me in bemusement.

"Master is such a sleepyhead!" She giggled and nuzzled up against my chest, purring softly.

"We were getting worried when you didn't so much as stir, even after the rest of us got up," Lily clarified. "I hope you don't mind – you looked like you were sleeping so peacefully, so maybe we shouldn't have..."

I gently pushed Nina down towards my lap so I could sit up properly. "No, no, it's fine – really." I offered Lily a tired smile, which seemed to help settle her concerns. However, as I looked to the end of the bed, I realized someone was missing. "Where's Luna?"

Lily gave a puzzled look. "Luna?"

"Oh, uh, the girl we brought back yesterday. She told me her name is Luna."

Nina gasped in awe. "Master! Nina didn't know you could understand her too!"

"No, no, at least – not any more than anyone else. She...I guess she came to me in my dreams last night. It's all kinda fuzzy, but I remember that much."

Lily gave a half-smile and took a spot on the side of the bed. "As soon as we all started getting up, she wandered downstairs and fell asleep on the couch. I think I overheard her mumble something about waiting for breakfast."

"Alright, guess I've slept in long enough anyway. I should go ahead and get started on that now–" I glanced up at Athena, who had been studying the three of us carefully. "Now that I think of it, I'm surprised you didn't say wake me up for training."

I gleaned the slightest hint of a blush before Athena quickly turned her back to us. "Yes, well, rest in and of itself is of as much import as physical exertion. A day's rest here and there will not meaningfully alter your development."

"Well now, I hope you're not going soft on me," I teased as I shifted Nina on to my shoulder and slid out of bed. She had apparently nodded off in the short time the rest of us were talking, and began to flail around ineffectively as she found herself in this new predicament.

Athena glanced back, narrowing her eyes.

"I can appreciate that manner of work ethic. Very well – follow me outside, we shall resume your instruction today."

With a sigh I placed Nina on the floor, who glared at me before walking away in a huff, and headed down to the backyard, bracing myself for what was to come.

Two hundred pushups? A five-mile run? Two straight hours of blade practice? I had been slowly growing accustomed to the rigors of training, but my mind swirled at what more Athena could throw at me. However, rather than firing out a command, she only offered a question.

"What do you know of the relation between hybrids and non-spirits?"

Her question betrayed none of its intention. Nina had been living with us for almost a month now, but she seemed to know as little about herself as anyone else.

"Almost nothing, I guess."

Athena closed her eyes and ran her hand across the top of her shield, which she had planted in the ground in front of her. She seemed to be struggling with whether to continue this line of conversation or not, though it only took her a few moments to make her decision.

"You are at least aware that certain individuals deign to capture and enslave these creatures as pets, correct?"

I thought back to when me and Lily first met Nina – the man

she was talking to, how she was separated from her mother, and how little she knew of where she even came from.

"Yeah, Nina told me as much when we first met. Or, uh, at least something like that, in her own very Nina way."

Athena bit her lip as her hand tightened into a fist. Although she was trying to maintain her composure, a tinge of anger scored each of her words.

"There are those who are neither beast nor spirit that inhabit the various realms outside this one," she continued. "They wield the one source of power that is able to most effectively harm these otherworldly beings – magic."

Athena seemed pained as she spoke, but I knew better than to interrupt.

"With their control of this power, they are able to bend creatures and, with proper mastery, even spirits to their will. Further, these mages are among the few beings to have garnered the ability to travel between realms."

A slight pause.

"You do understand the implications of this, no?"

Whitehearst's words suddenly came rushing back to me. *There will be dire consequences for your transgressions here.* I felt a cold sweat drip down the back of my neck as the pieces started to fall into place.

"I am afraid this goes well beyond the occasional creature or monster." Athena spoke softly, as if more to herself than to me. For the first time since meeting, I could sense genuine fear in her voice.

"Then...what should we do?"

When that man had given his ominous warning so many weeks ago, I didn't think twice about it; all I cared about was making sure Nina was safe. Even when he was gone, I doubted that we'd ever hear from him again, but now...now it seemed that was a very real possibility. Maybe even a certainty.

"What should we do?" I repeated.

I felt Athena place a hand on my shoulder and looked up, meeting a gaze filled with firm kindness. "I have asked much of you – perhaps more than any mortal should be burdened with. On this I cannot provide an answer, and only pledge my support to whatever path you should choose."

Was there even a choice to begin with? I suppose we could try to lay low, keep an eye on things, and just avoid trouble when it came our way. But then what kind of trouble could we even expect? And what would we do if it *did* find us?

There was so much I still didn't know, so much I couldn't do. Frustration began to well up inside right until I remembered Luna's words –

Who, not what.

These spirits – these girls – were my family now. We may not have known each other long, but they already meant the world to me. Even if they came from other realms, they were just like any other person...they wanted to learn, to grow, to find safety and happiness and companionship. I still wanted to get to know them, to go on adventures and share smiles and tears and hugs and mistakes. If someone wanted to threaten us – any of us – there was only one thing I could do.

"Please keep training me."

A gentle smile returned to Athena's lips. She nodded once more and moved to speak, but was cut off by a voice from behind.

"Me too."

Lily was standing in the doorway, ribbon undone and scythe in hand. I hadn't seen her holding that since her and Athena's...

confrontation, but her sure stare, coupled with the dull glean of the blade resting above her head, made her look like a completely different person from the meek, gentle girl I'd come to know.

"What do you mean?" I asked.

Lily stepped forward, her small stature contrasting with the size of her weapon as she leaned against it. "I won't let you face this alone. What– whatever it is."

Before I could respond, Lily turned her attention to Athena. "You understand, don't you?"

As their eyes locked, and this single moment melted into an eternity, Athena carefully studied Lily's features for… something. Fear? Hesitation? Doubt? She was the only one to know for sure.

Regardless, she at last seemed satisfied and let out a small sigh. "Very well. If circumstances progress to the worst of my suspicions, we will need the strength of each and every ally we can gather."

Lily gave a quick nod and took a step back as I brought out my sword, feeling its steady weight balance against the palm of my hand. Athena had been exacting in her instruction of the basics (so at least I had minimal risk of stabbing myself before my opponent), but we had never actually sparred together. My palms grew slick with nervous sweat, the hilt loosening ever so slightly in my grip. As I started to position my footing just like Athena had showed ("One foot forward, one step ready to be fallen back upon"), a streaming glint fell fast upon me.

With no time to think, I twisted the sword and braced my arm against the flat of the blade. Athena's weapon fell hard upon mine, the sudden impact sending me sprawling to the ground as the force of her blow continued to echo through my nerves.

As I tried to push myself back up, the muscles in my arms burning in protest, Athena crouched down and offered her hand.

"A commendable reaction," she said with the slightest hint of a smirk, pulling me to my feet. "The less of your mind devoted to your movements, the more it is free to plan ahead."

"I guess that has to count for something," I said with a weary smile, trying to massage away the lingering ache in my arms.

"If you truly want to learn, however, you must go beyond sheer instinct – you must make your weapon an extension of yourself, so that its movements are as natural and effortless as your own." Athena held her sword level against her body – it was a massive weapon, almost five feet in length, but she carried it with a gracefulness that made it appear weightless. "Come – try to attack me."

I glanced at Lily, hesitant. I trusted Athena well enough to not seriously injury me during training, but the thought of continuing to practice with *real* weapons seemed like a few steps ahead of where I was currently at.

"Worry not – no harm will become myself or you," Athena said gently. "Come now, and show me what you have learned."

Without much choice, I steadied myself again and took a quick step towards Athena. As I tried to land a blow from the side, she effortlessly turned her blade to mine and brushed it away. Riding on the forward momentum, I crouched down and launched myself back up, going for a thrust towards her center. Again, she returned the movement with a quick flit of her own, knocking my blade away.

This fruitless dance continued for several more strikes, as I approached from every angle I could think of, trying to throw her off in some way. Yet no matter what series of steps I applied, no matter what direction I came from, Athena seemed to easily predict my movements and act accordingly.

Winded, I dropped to the ground and looked up at her. "I yield," I wheezed, falling back in the grass and trying to catch my breath.

"Your turn," Athena said plainly, turning to Lily.

I propped myself back up, curious. Sure, she had a scythe and all, so it stood to reason that she must know *something* about using it. Plus, she had already saved me from that minotaur at school, so she was certainly a more capable fighter than me (though this was not a particularly high bar to clear).

Lily hopped to her feet and stood opposite Athena, the length of her scythe held at her side. She curtly nodded to Athena, signifying she was ready to spar.

Without another moment's hesitation, Athena held her sword high above and brought it down swiftly. Lily crouched slightly and held her weapon in both hands, letting the blow slide off as she loosened her right hand. With a light step forward, Lily reestablished her grip and swung for Athena's sword, catching it in the blade and forcing it low to the ground. Athena seemed caught off guard, if only for a second – she yanked back and swung for Lily's side, her nimble execution belying the sword's exceptional size.

Lily was still regaining her footing when she saw the swing coming, and tried to dive out of the way, though to no avail – as she was lying half on the ground, Athena poked her gently in the side.

"It would appear I still have plenty to teach you both yet." She helped Lily back to her feet and sheathed her sword, closing her eyes in concentration and murmuring to herself.

"You ok?" I whispered, eyeing where Athena had tapped Lily; she nodded and winced.

"I guess I'm still no match for her, huh?"

"That makes two of us," I responded, shaking my head.

Athena tucked in her skirt and sat down beside Lily, staring ahead past the yard and seemingly beyond to the horizon – the sun was making its ascent quickly, which meant it would be dark in only a few hours. For some reason I couldn't quite explain, I felt a chill come over me when I thought of this.

"I believe I know where to take your lessons from here," Athena said with an unexpected casualness. "Yuu–" I leaned forward to meet Athena's stern, yet soft, gaze. "You have no sense of bond with your weapon yet. It is plain that you have taken your training to heart, but any opponent with experience will easily predict your movements if you rely on learned techniques alone."

I balanced the sword on my knee, not sure how to respond.

"This is simple enough to rectify, in theory if not practice," Athena said with a reassuring smile. "Rely less on practiced movements, and more on your opponent's actions. The reason I was able to maintain the advantage was that you did not attempt to react to any of my movements – you only focused on your own style, and that is simple to read. We will work on watching your opponent and finding their weakness; only then will you be prepared for the challenges which most certainly lie ahead."

I gave a slow nod, trying to convince myself of my own resolve and stifle the anxiety welling within. If Athena was right, the only thing I could be sure of was that we – all of us here – would be facing a greater and more unknown danger than ever before. I had grown to care about these girls – in some way love them, even. But I couldn't say simply *wanting* to protect them would be enough to do so.

"And Lily..." Athena spoke with both fondness and pity. "Your technique is unpolished, as I expected, but what you lack in formal demonstration you supply well in fervor. We will work on the essentials together, and I believe you will be able to find your own way from there."

Lily clenched her fists and nodded to herself. As I watched the two continue to talk about things that were apparent and yet still so foreign, I realized that all these anxieties stemmed from one simple feeling – fear.

I had taken for granted up until now that all of us would be together as long as we wanted. But here we were, training to fight a threat we still knew so little about. When, where, how... these questions felt like they'd plague me until they resolved themselves in some terrible way. In such a relatively short time, I'd come to know each of them so much more intimately. And so I knew then I wasn't scared for myself – I was scared of what would happen to the girls who had, by some stroke of chance or fate, stumbled into my life and become such an integral part of it.

Despite Athena's training, despite the trust they'd placed in me, despite it all, I felt I had already let them down time and again. Both times we'd been attacked, I'd been useless or just got in the way, and put them in danger just trying save me.

But what could I do? I was just a regular, less-than-special human trying to understand, and even fight, beings from completely different worlds. The more I thought about it the more and more my mind continued to race...

"Yuu?"

With a start I snapped back to reality. Lily and Athena were looking over me with concern.

"Are you ok? You were staring off for some time and muttering to yourself."

Embarrassed, I shook my head and stood up. "Yeah, I'm fine, I just – sorry about that. Why don't we head back in? I haven't even made breakfast yet, and I'm sure Nina is waiting."

Although I knew I was a pretty terrible liar, Lily and Athena seemed to take me at my word and followed me inside. The best thing I could do for them was not become an even bigger burden than I already was. And so I would follow Athena's instruction – I would get stronger – and I would make sure I was for ready for whatever was coming.

19

"We have to join a what now?"

Himeo had slammed a stack of papers down, waking me from a critical morning nap.

"A club. As in an organization, here at school."

I waved her off, picking my head off the desk. "Yeah, yeah, I know what a club is. But why bring this up now?"

Himeo sighed and started playing with her bangs. "I figured you'd already know this, but before you graduate you have to have at least one extracurricular on record. Since we've only got one semester after this..." She narrowed her eyes as a familiar chill came over me. Whether this was from her glare or Lily scooching up next to me, I couldn't really say. "Get on it."

"Alright, alright. Thanks for looking out for me," I mumbled, picking up one of the forms and looking it over – as expected, it was overrun with the usual overwrought bureaucracy the student council was known for. Though from what I was able to gather, this was nowhere near as bad as before Himeo joined; she had apparently helped streamline or even eliminate a lot of the more overbearing school policies, which earned her a gracious (if unstated) thanks from much of the student body.

"So which do you think we should join?"

"That's for you to decide. If you need ideas, the school is hosting a recruitment fair later today – if you go, you're bound to see at least one or two you like. Plus, you can have the club leader fill everything out right there, so it's one less thing to worry about."

I glanced at Lily, who had been resting her head on my shoulder and reading over the form. "What do you think? Should we just take our chances then?"

"Let's go! It'll be fun to see everyone doing their best," she said cheerily, before blushing faintly. "A-and I'd be happy doing anything with you."

I tussled Lily's hair. "Alright, sounds like a plan. Will we see you there?"

Himeo shook her head. "I have another meeting after school, but I'm sure you'll be fine." She bent down towards Lily and whispered loud enough for me to hear. "By the way, make sure you take good care of him for me, alright?"

"You can count on me," Lily said with a serious nod.

Himeo stood back up, satisfied, as both girls retook their seats just in time for the morning bell.

* * *

To my relief, the rest of the day continued on with a refreshing sense of mundanity.

It seemed like just as I had started settling into my new life – spirits, monsters, and otherworldly powers alike – even greater threats were brewing just on the horizon, so the chance to set all those worries aside for even one day was a welcome respite. And while each class blurred into the next, the end of the school day snuck upon me and found me and Lily making our way to the first floor, where an endless flow of students, stalls, and streamers filled the halls and adjacent courtyard. Despite the chaotic nature of the event itself, there was an unmistakable organization to the layout that kept the frenzied energy somewhat self-contained – all the sports teams were placed at the front, followed by subject interest groups, and miscellaneous organizations eking out past that.

"See anything you like so far?" I asked as Lily and I tried to squeeze between two masses of students signing up for the soccer and volleyball teams.

"It's…it's a bit much to take in all at once," she replied, struggling to push her way through. I reached out my hand and helped yank her past, granting us some much-needed space to catch our breath and take a closer look at the surrounding tables.

While club leaders and new recruits alike were calling out from every direction for any and all to join, no specific clubs were jumping out at us. And to be fair, it was hard to feel invested in a club I knew I'd only be a part of for about a semester or so – another casualty of my perpetual procrastination in all things school-related, I supposed.

After winding this way and that through a maze of students and stalls, I found a rare opening in the crowd and stepped aside with Lily, exasperated. "It just doesn't seem like there's any place that's a good fit for us," I murmured. "There's the history club –"

"But you have to be able to commit at least a full year," she finished softly. "There was the anime club though – !"

"But they're already maxed out on members," I added with resignation.

I leaned against the wall and let out a sigh. "Do you think

we'll really find anything here? I know it'll only be for a few months, so we could probably make do with anything, but…" I slumped down. "I dunno, it'd feel like a waste if we didn't pick something at least a little interesting."

Lily squatted down next to me and placed a hand on my shoulder. "Cheer up! We still haven't seen every club that's here, right? We can't lose hope yet." Her gentle smile was infectious, and as I picked myself back up, I felt my mood rising in kind.

"Yeah, you're right – there's no sense in getting all depressed now. It may even be a chance to try something totally new." I offered my hand and helped Lily up as we continued through the labyrinth of multicolored balloons, decorated tables, and signboards reaching out from every side.

As we passed by the astrology club, however, I spotted what looked like a familiar face – a small girl with short, brown hair, sitting alone at a table filled with fliers and books. It wasn't unusual for some clubs to be way more popular than others, but the fact that not a single other person was even looking her way or helping out made her stand out all the more.

I nudged Lily and pointed towards the lonesome girl. "Hey, is that – ?"

Lily glanced back and, as soon as she caught sight of who I was looking at, sped ahead. "It is! Let's go say hi!" She grabbed my hand and pulled me over, almost sending me tumbling into the gardening club's table (as well as their assortment of very sharp, very pointy tools).

"Mae!" Lily shouted cheerily, giving a quick bow. "We haven't seen you since the festival! Do you remember us?"

The girl seemed perplexed for just a moment, before recognition spread across her face and she beamed back at us. "Oh, um...Hi! You're Jun's friends, right?"

"More or less," I said, finally having regained my footing. Even with Lily's "gift", I'd prefer to keep the number of holes in my body to a minimum.

"What are you doing here all alone?" Lily asked, looking around. "Isn't there anyone else helping you?"

Mae picked up a flier and gestured to the poster on her table forlornly. "It's what it looks like. No one's interested in joining." She hesitated. "But I guess I shouldn't be surprised – it's been like this ever since I took over the club. Even the seniors who graduated last year had trouble getting any new members, so it's probably not just me." She held her gaze on the flier in her hand. "...Right?"

"Well, what kind of club is this, anyway?" I asked, scouring over the table's contents. There were the usual registration forms each club had handy, plus a smattering of books that ranged from crisp spines and glossy fronts to deteriorating pages just hanging on by the friction of its covers. The cracked leather binding on one such book was particularly noticeable, given that there appeared to be no title or author anywhere on it.

Mae tapped her fingers together nervously, her eyes not daring to meet mine or Lily's. "It's, uh..." She began to stammer, and seemed like she was about to finish her sentence before mumbling something inaudible.

"I'm sorry?"

"The oc..."

"Ock?"

"THE OCCULT CLUB," Mae blurted suddenly, before turning red and clasping her hands over her mouth. Lily and I looked at each other before turning back to Mae, who hung her head, sullen.

"You probably think it's dumb and weird, don't you?"

I picked up one of the fliers lying in a stack on the table and scanned it over. "Not really, especially considering I don't know anything about it. What do you do?"

As if a switch had been flipped, Mae's entire demeanor changed, filled with an until-this-point absent energy.

"You mean you'll join?" she asked with an intense stare.

"Well, uh, I was just asking what you do, y'know? What's your club all about?"

Mae sunk back into her chair, the excitement gone from her voice. "Oh, right. That paper should be able to explain it better than I can."

I took a closer look at the flier – INTERESTED IN SECRETS UNKNOWN? CURIOUS ABOUT MYSTERIES BEYOND THE REALM OF HUMAN COMPREHENSION? JOIN THE OCCULT CLUB TODAY ~ ANSWERS LIE WITHIN.

"It certainly sounds, uh, interesting." I still wasn't sure I understood what this club was really all about, let alone how to react to it.

"So what do you think?" Mae asked softly.

Before I could respond, Lily grabbed Mae's hands in her own. "It sounds perfect!"

"It does?" Mae asked in a tone not dissimilar from my own.

Lily nodded. "We need a club we can both join, but we've been worried we wouldn't fit in with any of the other groups. If you're willing to have us, we'd be happy to sign up."

Mae looked from me, to Lily, and back to me, searching for some kind of confirmation.

"Uh, yeah, sure. Could be fun, right?"

Mae was blushing fiercely as she quickly grabbed some

papers and began hacking away at them furiously. "Don't worry about signing up I'll take care of all the annoying administrative stuff for you I've never done this before but I've practiced a lot just in case because I wanted to make sure I did it right in case anyone *did* join not that it happened before but now that it has I should take responsibility so I'll just need you two to fill out these last few bits and then we'll be all set!"

Lily offered a pitying smile to me as she shrugged and began to fill out the rest of her form; with little other choice, I followed suit.

"So, Mae?" The girl shot her head back up from the page she was pouring over, her eyes fixed on me intently. "When's the first meeting?"

"We can have it right after this!" She clapped her hands together excitedly, but then seemed to remember something. "If you don't mind helping me clean up a bit first, that is. I hate to ask for your help on the same day you join, but, um..." She paused, searching for a follow-up. "It'd give me a chance to tell you a little more about what we – or, uh, I – do!"

"It's no problem, we're full-fledged members of the club now, right? We'll think of this like our first official club activity." Lily gave a swift nod as the two of us set to work gathering the eclectic mix of items on the table, sorting and piling things up as needed.

For what it was worth, there wasn't too much organizing that needed to be done afterwards, given that we seemed to be the only people to have stopped by in the first place. Other than a few papers shuffled around and what appeared to be a beat-up encyclopedia opened up to some random page, the table was in immaculate shape. And so, with stacks of books and forms in hand, we followed Mae as she dropped off our registration sheets at the student council office and headed over to our new club room together.

"I'm sorry it's so out of the way," Mae said sheepishly as we trekked through the third floor hallway. As all the excitement of the recruitment fair still seemed to echo through the rest of the school, the near-silence we faced up here was somewhat unsettling.

"It's no problem, it's not like you chose where to put it, right?"

A shock seemed to pass over Mae, as she paused briefly before continuing forward. "Well, uh, you see…"

"Oh?" Lily asked, catching up to Mae's position.

"The club leaders *do* choose their own rooms, but they're given priority based on membership. Even when we were at our biggest, it was only a few of us, or so I heard…" Mae seemed more disappointed in herself than the actual situation.

"At least it's quiet up here, right?" Lily said earnestly, to which Mae gave a cautious nod. "And look at the view!" She ran over to a large window opposite the rows of classrooms stretching ever-onward. "You could even watch the sun set every day, that's wonderful." She closed her eye and smiled blissfully, lost in her own senses.

"I-I guess it's not all bad," Mae said with a weak smile. "Oh, here we are."

At the very end of the hallway stood a splintering door, its darkened woodgrain and rust-speckled doorknob indicating its age as much as neglect. I'd say this singular door stood out in comparison, if it weren't for the fact that you'd be hard-pressed to notice it even while standing right next to it.

"Well, shall we?" Mae turned the nob gingerly, as rusty gears shifted into place and worn-out hinges groaned in protest.

As we entered the room, one thing struck me immediately

– it was entirely plain. I guess I didn't know *what* to expect with an "Occult Club", but boring certainly wasn't it. The room itself had little in the way of furnishings or decorations – just a single cabinet placed in the corner, and a few chairs scattered about. I moved to ask why the club room had so little in it, but just as quickly found the answer as I considered the three of us standing here.

"So, Mae?" I stepped further into the room, with Lily right behind me. "What kinda stuff do you do in here?"

When I was met with a stifling silence, I glanced back to see if everything was ok – I would've felt terrible if I somehow offended our new club leader on the same day we joined.

"Y-u…" Mae was standing in front of the doorway, her head hung and her words barely audible.

"Me?" I looked to Lily for confirmation, but she seemed as confused by the situation as I was.

"Y-u." Mae spoke a little louder this time, but I still couldn't make out exactly what she was trying to say.

"Uh, yep. That's me." I laughed nervously, trying to relieve some of the tension that was welling up inside the room.

Mae began to step towards me, finally raising her head. The look in her eyes was…different, yet still somehow so familiar.

"You feeling ok? I know it's probably been a long day for you what with all the excitement earlier so we can just leave if you'd like–"

Before I could finish, Mae had closed the gap between us and grabbed my shirt, lifting it up and in front of my face. For how small she was, she had a surprisingly good reach.

"Uh, not for nothing, but could you tell me what's going on?"

"It IS you!" She declared, her voice filled with a frightening intensity. I had to be somewhat thankful that she was still holding the bottom of my shirt in front of me so I couldn't see what kind of expression she wore while saying that.

"Um, Mae, can you please put Yuu's shirt down now? I don't think he likes that." I could hear Lily from my side, carefully trying to reason with our quite-possibly-insane new friend.

"Oh! Oh? Oh. Oh..." Mae's voice had returned to its normal (or whatever was actually "normal" for this girl), soft cadence, as she loosened her grip and let my shirt fall back against my body. "I-I...I can explain, I promise."

Despite her rather abrupt change in demeanor, I could still sense the sincerity in her voice.

"Sure, sure, no harm done." I tried to pat out the creases in my shirt as Lily grabbed some chairs from the side of the room, the metallic screeching as they slid along the floor giving pause to any further conversation.

"So what got you all excited in the first place? I know we met before, but didn't we go over that already?"

Mae's eyes darted back and forth across the floor, her face still a deep red. I wasn't sure if what I was feeling was pity or sheer bewilderment.

"You were the one who saved me...a few months ago. I knew it was you."

"Saved? How?" I wracked my brain trying to think of when I might've seen Mae before, but the only recollection I had was our brief introduction at the Lunar Festival. Other than that – nothing.

"I was walking home after school, when I was chased by – by...something. I – I don't know what it was, or why it was coming after me, but I just remember – " She took a deep breath, trying to steady her voice. "I remember hearing some terrible scream, and when I turned around, there you were on the ground. You were…you were dead. I know you were. I – I – "

"I'm not sure what you saw," I interjected with as neutral a tone as I could hold. "But that couldn't have been me. I mean, I'm sitting right here in front of you now, aren't I?"

"That's right," Lily added, leaning forward to meet Mae's gaze. "Maybe what you saw was – "

"No!" Mae clenched her hands together on her lap. "No, I – I know it was you. I'll never forget it, I – " The tears she had tried to choke back were welling up again. "I saw you die. I *saw* it. Why won't you believe me?"

I hesitated, trying to choose my next words carefully.

"It's not that I don't believe you, it's just – " I waved my hand in the air, trying to think of some explanation that would satisfy her. "That's a lot to take in all of the sudden, y'know? Like – "

Finally, a thread to latch on to.

"Like maybe it was just someone who looked like me. Whatever happened, whatever you saw must've been traumatizing, so it'd be easy to mistake – "

"I know it was you." Mae had regained her composure, at least partially. "I – I can prove it."

Lily and I remained silent as Mae traced the outline of the symbol on my chest in the air. She repeated this motion several times before bringing her hands together once more.

"Do you believe me now?"

I felt the weight of the question bearing down on me. So far the only people who knew of how I died were my closest friends and housemates. As a new threat seemed to be looming large on the horizon, I had to even more seriously consider who I let know about Lily, Nina, and Athena's true nature.

"Do you think I'm crazy?" she added quietly.

"Just a li–mmph."

Before I could finish, Lily had gently covered my mouth with her hand, shaking her head slowly as I tried to protest.

"Mae, what do you think I am?"

I watched Lily carefully, uncertainty still abounding. Mae *seemed* harmless enough, if more than a little eccentric, but there was still so little we understood about why spirits had started showing up, or what role Nina's former "master" might be playing in all this. And yet, as each beat of my heart reverberated against the walls of the room, I knew I had to place my trust in Lily, just like she had done for me.

"You're…not human, are you?" Mae spoke to the ground, unwilling – or perhaps unable – to meet our gaze now.

Each second took another breath away as I waited for Lily to respond.

"You're right, I'm not."

"And that…mark…on his chest?"

Lily nodded. "It's a seal."

"So you really are –?"

Lily smiled contentedly. "Yes, I'm a spirit."

Mae was unmoving, frozen in her contemplative position. Just as I was about to reach out and ask if she was ok, she leapt to her feet and pointed at me and Lily in turn.

"Aha! I knew it! I couldn't tell anyone before but I was sure there was something weird going on and now I finally have proof I have so many questions you have to tell me all about where you came from who you are what happened how you met I can't wai–"

"Sh-she sure is an energetic one," Lily said with a nervous laugh.

"Mae," I said as calmly as I could. The past few minutes were a whirlwind, and this mood whiplash wasn't helping. "How do you know about spirits in the first place?"

"Oh, right!"

Mae scurried over to the dilapidated cabinet tucked away in the corner and threw open the doors, revealing two neat stacks of books of varying condition and size. It seems what she had on her table during the club fair was just a sampling of the small library she had packed away here. Running her finger down the rows of spines, Mae appeared engrossed in her search, until she finally grabbed a single volume from the column and deftly pulled it out, setting it on her chair for us to see.

"What kind of book is this?" I asked.

The cover had definitely seen better days, with most of the material ripped or worn away. The pages themselves were sticking out in every direction, and the whole binding seemed to be on its last legs. I honestly couldn't tell if this was all due to age or simply a lack of care for the thing.

"Not just any book – a guide on all things mystical and magical." Mae opened the tome, flipping through pages as she spoke.

"And…that's how you learned about spirits?"

"Mhm! Not just spirits – all manner of monsters and creatures and artifacts that don't come from this world. Look –" She stopped flipping and pointed to a simple image on a crisped yellow page. "Look familiar?"

A circle overlaying a triangle…the same thing that appeared on my chest after I first met Lily.

"What do you know about it?"

Mae looked up and tapped her chin. "Not much, honestly. The only thing this book told us is that this marks a human who has made a deal with a spirit. I haven't been able to find any more information...It's why I got a bit, um –" She paused and glanced at me and Lily. "Excited earlier. I was hoping you could tell me more about it."

I sighed and shook my head. "I could say the same thing at this point, really. Everything I know comes from her." I gestured towards Lily.

"And I'm afraid even I lack the knowledge you're interested in," Lily finished.

"O-oh, I'm sorry," Mae said dejectedly.

For as strange as she had shown herself to be, I was starting to believe that Mae might actually know quite a bit about where the spirits and monsters were coming from, as well as –

"What happened on that day?"

"Pardon?" Mae looked up from the book with surprise, as if pulled from her own separate world.

"That day, when...when I died. If you were really there, then can you tell me what you saw?" I considered whether this was pushing her too much, but I didn't want the opportunity to slip away. "Anything you can remember would help."

"I – " Mae hesitated, then took a deep breath. "I'm not sure. I remember going home the same way I do every day, and when I turned a corner there was...was *something* standing in front of me, like it was waiting."

"Can you remember what it looked like?"

"My memory's still hazy..." Mae clutched her sleeves and shuddered. "But I know it wasn't human. It – it couldn't be. Up until now I thought it had to have just been my imagination, that everything until now was just some weird dream, but – "

She looked from me to Lily as she placed her hands back on the tome in front of her.

"Now I know that's not the case."

"So what happened next? I think I saw you running past, but – "

"What else could I do? That thing was huge! And it – "

Mae cut herself off as she hurriedly flipped through the book, eagerly searching for something. After a brief attempt, however, she sighed in resignation.

"Never mind, it's no good. It's like it's on the tip of my mind, but the harder I try to remember the further away it gets."

"But…you do remember it chasing you, right?" Lily ventured.

"Yeah, I mean – I think it had to be? I didn't exactly turn around to check, since all I heard was this growl, or roar, or – "

"So…" Lily interrupted gently. "That means it wanted something from you."

"But if that's the case, then why'd it go after me?" I asked.

"Maybe you got in the way?" Lily said plainly. "If it was acting on instinct alone, then it might've attacked you to get to her."

Mae slowly shook her head side to side, staring at her lap with a blank expression.

"Er – I guess that's all we know for now," I said with a forced chuckle. "But hey, about that book in front of you – "

Mae snapped back to attention and gripped the cover.

"Hm? This? What about it?"

"It's just, uh, you mentioned something about an 'us' when you were talking earlier. Who were you talking about?"

Mae let out a small laugh. "Oh, that. Just the seniors before me – they were the ones that introduced me to this club. They were…they were my first friends."

She looked at the page wistfully, tracing her finger over a creature that could only be described as a mess of bone and sinew.

"We've never had any official funding, so we had to buy all these things ourselves. I remember finding this with them when we went looking through a secondhand store. It shouldn't have been any different from the other books that we have, but something about it felt...different." She turned back to us and smiled in embarrassment. "That probably sounds pretty weird, huh?"

I wanted to point out that this was hardly the strangest thing she had said today alone, but I decided to follow my better judgment and keep my mouth shut.

"Not at all," Lily said with a reassuring smile. "I know few humans who truly believe in the sorts of spirits and monsters that seem to be written here. The fact that you do nonetheless is something special."

"T-thanks." Mae nodded to herself and closed the book carefully. "I'm sorry this didn't exactly go how I wanted, but, um..." She hesitated, gathering her courage. "You'll still come back next week, right?"

Lily and I glanced at each other, then turned back to Mae.

"Of course, prez."

"I'm sure there's plenty still we can teach other," Lily added.

Mae offered one last smile and nodded, as I held the door open for the two of them. Our newest friend may have been more than a little eccentric, but her arcane knowledge would prove to be an invaluable asset before long.

19

"Hey, Nina?" I wandered into the living room, finding her curled up in a ball on the couch. She lifted her head groggily, ears twitching slightly.

"Hm? What is it master?"

I sat down in an adjacent chair and smoothed down the stray hairs that were sticking out this way and that. "I was wondering if you'd wanna go out with me today?"

Nina's cheeks flushed a deep pink as she began to stammer. "M-m-me? You want to go on a date with N-Nina?"

"Uh, I'm not quite sure I'd call it a date," I said with some embarrassment, but Nina was already lost in her own thoughts.

"Nina always wanted to go on a date with master, but so soon? Is she ready? Is this too much, oh Nina doesn't know –"

"Nina? Niiina?" I waved my hand in front of her face, trying to bring her back to reality.

"Huh? Oh? What?" As she finally snapped out of it, Nina began bowing her head repeatedly. "Sorry master, sorry. Um… " She looked back at me, her brown eyes betraying their true depths in the reflection of the afternoon sun. "Nina would love to go wherever you want, if you'll have her."

"Of course! Now let's see…"

I stood up and stretched, checking the clock – it was only

2:00 PM, but since it got dark pretty early this time of year, it'd be prudent to leave soon.

"You ok with heading out in just a few minutes? That should give us plenty of time before it gets too cold out."

Nina nodded and bounded to her feet, before holding out her hands. "Wait right here – Nina just remembered something." Before I had a chance to respond, she had dashed around the corner and up the stairs, the soft tapping of her feet against the floor the only indication as to her direction.

"My room?" I wondered aloud.

Lily had already gone out with Himeo earlier in the day (for some much-needed "girl-to-girl" time, the latter told me – though since she was already living in a house full of almost nothing *but* girls, I was a bit perplexed by the notion), Athena was out in the backyard working on her garden, so that only left –

"Back!" Nina had returned in no time at all with Luna leaning on her shoulder, her gentle, steady breathing indicating that she was still fast asleep.

"Er – not to be rude, but why'd you bring Luna down with you?"

"To come with us, silly! Nina asked if she wanted to go see the city as well, and she said yes. So she can come with us, right master?" Nina stared at me with wide, pleading eyes – even a heart made of stone would crack under that adorable pressure.

"Sure, sure – there's just one problem."

"Oh?"

I tapped Luna on the head softly, eliciting a small mumble. "I don't think she's planning on waking up anytime soon – it'd be kind of hard to walk around together if she lacks the whole 'walking' part."

Nina giggled and waved my arm away. "That's easy! Master can just carry her, right?"

I looked from Luna, to the clock, and back at Luna again. It's true I had already carried her all the way home from the festival that one night, and she *was* surprisingly light, even for her small frame. My only concern was *how much* walking we'd be doing, but...

"Ah, why not." I bent down and held my arms behind me. "Can you help her climb on?"

Nina gingerly repositioned so that Luna was able to lean onto me as I grabbed her legs and hoisted her up. As I got ready to move her arms around my shoulders, I felt a small pair of lips brush against my cheek while a barely perceptible "Thank you" drifted past.

Surprised, I turned to see if Luna was finally awake – but given that her eyes were still closed and breathing as even and undisturbed as ever, I could only chalk the whole thing up to my overactive imagination.

"Well then, ready to go?" I asked as I re-secured Luna on my back. Nina gave an energetic cheer and grabbed my arm, clinging tight. As the three of us ventured towards the city, I held no doubts that our happy little group was quite the sight to behold.

* * *

"Wooooah!" Nina was bounding up and down as we passed rows of apartments and stores tightly packed against (and sometimes on top of) one another. "People *live* here?"

"Mhm, quite a lot of people. That's why they make these buildings so tall – so many people live and work here, they need to use every little bit of space they have."

Nina's mouth was agape as she whipped her head around, trying to take in all the colossal structures that surrounded us.

"While it's fun to visit," I continued as I guided Nina along, "I think living here would be too much for me."

"Nina wouldn't mind..." I felt her petite frame press against my arm as she squeezed tight. "As long as master was there." Lacking the ability to give her a proper response, I nudged her cheek gently with my arm, a token of my own affection.

"I'm a bit surprised though," I said as we dodged a pair of besuited men hurrying past and sharing a packet of papers between them. "Wasn't this the place you arrived at when you first came to this world?"

"Umm, Nina guesses, but, but – " She shook her head emphatically. "She didn't know what any of it really was. Being here with Y– I mean, master, is like seeing it all for the first time!"

"You know you can just call me Yuu, right?" I asked with a concerned smile. "In fact I think it'd probably be bet– "

"No, no! Nina – Nina couldn't do that." Her typically airy voice held a new gravity as she spoke. "Master is master, and Nina is Nina."

I leaned into Nina as a jogger in bright shorts came sprinting past. "Yeah, but Yuu is Yuu too, right?"

"Nina – " She hesitated, as if considering a crossroads set before her. "Master is master, and Nina is Nina," she quietly repeated.

"Then what about your previous master?" Nina's ears straightened back up, her attention sparked anew. "Gregory Whitehearst, right?"

"Nina...was, but, but – why are you asking about him? You're not going to send Nina back, are y–"

"No, no, no – I would never. In fact, it's just the opposite." I led her over to a nearby bench and sat Luna down next to me, resting her head on my shoulder. "Athena thinks there's a chance he may try to find you and take you back. And I won't let that happen." I offered what I hoped was a reassuring smile. "None of us will."

Nina's fingers curled around the hem of her skirt as she stared at the ground.

"You won't?"

"Never." I reached out and pet her head slowly. "But that's why I need your help. Maybe Athena's wrong, and I really hope she is, but I want to be prepared just in case anything *does* happen. And since you lived with Whitehearst for some time, I thought you might –"

"No."

"Huh?"

Nina stood in front of me, tears welling in her eyes. "Nina won't. She can't. Master, you– you can't..." Before I could reach out again, she bolted down the sidewalk, her speed far exceeding anything I could hope to match.

I tried to call out to her, but she didn't so much as look back. Without much recourse, I ran after her, trying to not rustle Luna too much; even knowing what a heavy sleeper she was, I still felt bad for jostling her around.

I continued my pursuit as I turned this way and that, always catching Nina just out of the corner of my eye. Even as my chest heaved and lungs burned, I called out to her time and again, though it didn't take long for her to completely disappear from my sight. Still, I couldn't just give up. For as fast as she'd ran away, I was sure she that once she thought she'd lost us she'd relax – I had brought up a pretty sensitive topic out of the blue, so I could only hope she just needed a few moments to herself.

Slowing my pace to a light jog, I stopped to lean against the corner of a nearby building and thought about where Nina might've ran off to. I had my doubts that she'd just run away aimlessly, so it was likely she went somewhere she was somewhat familiar with. And if memory served, the only place that fit that description was…

Without another moment's hesitation I changed course and cut through a nearby alley, weaving through tightly packed walls and scattered junk in mostly-forgotten corners. I knew this was still nothing more than an educated guess, but it was all I had to go on.

Now what must've only taken a few minutes felt like hours, each second ticking away nurturing the fear that I may not actually find Nina – that my guess would be wrong, and the city itself would swallow her, never to return. However, as I crashed through one last alleyway, spilling over a set of bushes meant to block the less-than-pristine imagery it created, I found her.

"Nina!" I panted, only able to let out her name before collapsing into a fit of wheezing and choking.

"Master? H-how did you know?" Nina was standing in front of the arcade we had first met at, still not out of place among the costumed attendants.

"I-I knew…that you…didn't know…the city…that well, so…" I had to stop again to catch my breath. "So you'd come…to the one place…you knew." Exhausted, I cradled Luna in front of me and slumped against the alleyway wall.

"Master…"

Once more I met Nina's gaze – her wide brown eyes still

brimming with tears and bearing plain her feelings. "You can't!"

Nina leapt towards my chest, squeezing Luna between us and knocking me back against the wall.

"Hey, it's ok, it's all ok." I freed one of my arms and began to pet Nina's head, her grip tightening onto my sleeve as she buried her face against it.

For some time we just stood there together, absent from the world around us. The flow of Nina's silent tears abated, and at last she pulled away.

"Master…you won't, right?"

"I – "

"Nina overheard everyone talking about her old master… They said – master said – they're going to fight him." She balled her hands and gently hit against my chest. "Nina can't lose her master, she can't lose her family, you said, you said–"

Before she could finish, Nina broke out into another muted cry and hid her face once more. Just as I was about to comfort her, a hand reached out in front of me and caressed Nina's ear.

"There…there…" The voice was soft and light, and had the faintest tinge of familiarity to it. "He…will be…ok…" Looking down, I found my suspicions confirmed – Luna was actually talking, her pale violet eyes just barely perceptible as she continued to stroke Nina's head. "You'll…be there…when he… needs you…right?"

Wiping away her tears, Nina nodded firmly. As precious as the whole exchange was, the weight of Luna's words were not lost on me – despite how much I felt I relied on them, these girls had, in many ways, come to rely on me just the same. I had a responsibility to protect them not just physically, but emotionally as well.

"That's a…good girl…So no more…tears…now." With one

last yawn, Luna drew her arm back to my shoulder and rested her head against my neck. "Goodnight everyone~"

Hearing Luna's steady breathing return once more, I turned back to Nina, who was staring at me intently.

"I'm...sorry about before, I didn't mean to spring that on you so suddenly –"

Nina shook her head fiercely. "Mm mm, Nina shouldn't have run away like that. She was just scared..." She paused, as a hundred different thoughts seemed to run across her mind. "But...she won't run again. Not anymore."

Tenderly taking my hand, she placed it against the top of her chest. I could feel a soft, rhythmic beating as she placed her own hand over mine.

"Nina can't bond with master like the others...She can't give him a special gift or help him fight. But she loves master just as much as the others – e–even more maybe!" With a cheeky smile she hopped back and threw her arms up. "So master has to look out for Nina too, ok?"

Careful to keep Luna steady in my arms, I laughed and got to my feet. "You have my word. As long as we're together, I won't let anything bad happen to you."

Shadows were starting to crawl along the walls of the surrounding buildings, and the air began to nip at our cheeks.

"But hey, since we already came all the way out here, why don't we do something fun before it gets too late? Plus, there's still a lot I want to learn about you, if you don't mind sharing."

Nina clung to my arm and nuzzled her cheek against me, purring softly. "Of course Nina will follow master wherever he goes! But where to begin..."

As Nina began to describe her earliest memories of childhood, we continued down the street amid a mass of people, the final rays of a falling sun racing to meet us.

20

"And then, and then that's when Nina first saw the outside, and that's when she – "

As the three of us continued our impromptu "date", Nina told me a little more about where she came from. Since she had been born and raised in captivity, her mom had been her only real companion through most of her life, though she disappeared a few years before Nina showed up in our own world here. Whitehearst himself treated her as an equal parts pet and maid, and forbade from ever leaving the manor grounds. Nina explained that while he never *directly* hurt her, he had more than enough menace to keep her from ever thinking of escaping – and even if she somehow did get away, she had nowhere else to go. The only solace she could take was in her mother's care, and a childhood friend who snuck in to visit when she could. Apparently this friend was also a hybrid, though she stopped seeing Nina right around the time her mom went missing.

"It must've been lonely like that, trapped in a room all by yourself..." The streets were starting to fill with other passerby again, the transition to the nighttime crowd slowly making its adjustment.

Nina looked up, then shook her head. "Not really – at least, not when Nina's momma and Ruby were around. Even if it was a little scary when they went away…" She looked forlorn for just a moment, before perking up again. "Now she has a new home! And you'll help Nina find her momma, right?"

"R-right." I forced a smile and pressed on, trying not to dwell on the fact that I had no clue who her mom was or where she could possibly be. "So do you remember anything about Whitehearst? Anything you think we should know?"

"He's really strong…" Nina spoke just above a whisper, as if afraid he'd hear her. "Nina never saw him use magic, but she knows he's one of the strongest mages from her world."

A grim look clouded her expression, so I gently nudged her and offered a reassuring smile.

"That's why I'll just have to get stronger, right? For you, for me – for all of us." Nina gave a weak smile in return and nodded, as some of the dark thoughts hovering around her seemed to clear.

As I returned my attention to the street ahead, I noticed a tiny shop inlaid from the other surrounding buildings. It was mostly unremarkable save for a worn, metal sign half-clung to the wall, the word "ANTIQUES" only barely visible after years of battling the elements.

"Hey, do you wanna check out that store for a little?" Nina looked over and her eyes widened.

"Wooooah, what kind of place is that?" She shifted her attention from the store to me and back again as we approached, bounding in place with each step.

"They sell all kinds of old things at these shops, so you never really know what you'll find. I thought it might be fun to look around and see what we stumble across."

Nina gave a cheer of approval as she now dragged me towards the door, her excitement having finally gotten the better of her.

20

As the rusted metal door clanged behind us, I had a chance to take a decent survey of the store. It was a small shop, made all the smaller due to the rows of items stacked up on shelves that almost touched the ceiling in every part of the room, creating a makeshift maze to wander through. Every way I looked I was greeted with new oddities that chirped and glinted and boasted intricate handiwork by craftsmen long-forgotten. It was as if I was walking through the halls of human history itself, not the kind written about in books and remembered by most, but the raw, personal history of daily life. It was a curious feeling, but an altogether not-unpleasant one.

Nina, for her part, seemed to be enjoying this treasure trove of trinkets just as much. She carefully inspected each metallic piece she came across, and giggled with surprise and delight as a music box began to play when she opened it. Even Luna must've been having some fun herself, as I could hear what sounded like a faint laugh interjected in her soft, even breathing.

As I was looking over a grey stuffed rabbit sitting on a doll chair tucked away in the corner, I felt a light tap on my shoulder. With some effort I was able to turn around, trying to be careful not to knock anything over with my extra passenger in tow. An elderly man was stooped in front of me, a tiny pair of round spectacles sitting toward the bottom of his nose. He had a few tufts of white hair neatly combed to the side, and donned a wine red vest over his white button-up. When he saw that he had my attention, he smiled warmly and gestured towards Nina, who was playing with a few bird miniatures that cheeped when you moved them.

"Is that your girlfriend, young man?" he asked.

"Oh, uh, her? No, no – I mean, she's just my friend, and –"

"Say no more, say no more." The man waved his hands and laughed to himself, as if he had heard this kind of thing a thousand times before. "I know how these things go, don't fret. Why don't you come with me for just a minute?" I watched as he shuffled away and, figuring I had nothing to lose, followed shortly after.

The man stopped by the back of the store, where an assortment of jewelry and watches were laid out in a glass case. Although there didn't seem to be a clear organization to the collection, the mishmash of shine and wear, bright and dull, glimmering and rusted created a phantasmic projection of colors onto the glass itself.

"She's a sweet one, isn't she?" the man said as he bent down behind the counter.

I glanced back at Nina as she carefully cupped her hands around one of the birds, cooing at it as if it were the real thing. "Yeah, she's...she's really something."

"Not too many kids these days appreciate the simpler things like we have here –" The man stood up and – seeming to have remembered something quite suddenly – gave a wheezing laugh. "You'll have to forgive me – you all are too old to rightly be considered kids now, aren't you? But for an old-timer like me, it's hard not to see all you young'n's like that." He ducked back behind the counter, a chorus of rustling and jangling accompanying his second bout of laughter.

"Ah, yeah, she's not from around here, so I guess this is all pretty new to her."

Watching Nina's left ear twitch as she held a wooden box close to her face, looking for the latch that would release the two halves of the piece from each other, I tried to capture the moment in eternity. If I could give her that – a reprieve from the sadness, the fear, the uncertainty she had lived with for so long – I'd be happy.

The old man grumbled something that I took to be consensus, before finally standing up once more and placing a golden bell in front of me. The piece itself was unassuming, a deep bronze hue masking whatever shine it may have otherwise held long ago.

"It's a pretty little thing, isn't it?" The man – who it seemed clear by now was either the shop owner or a very brazen customer – gave a proud grin as he picked up the bell and shook it. "Missing the clapper, but it'd make a nice gift for a special girl all the same, don'tcha think?"

I gave a nervous laugh. "Uh, yeah, it sure would." I understood what he was getting at, but it'd take too long to explain what our actual relationship was – *whatever* our actual relationship was.

The owner sighed as he turned the bell over in his hand, as if picking apart each tiniest detail. "This little guy has been sitting here for lord knows how many years – it'd feel a waste to let it stay even longer. What say you take it off my hands for me?"

"It really is nice…" I shifted an arm out from under Luna to take a closer look at the ornament as well – I had to admit, the owner had good taste, and it would fit perfectly on Nina. Placing the bell back down, I reached into my pocket to retrieve my wallet, but the result was…less than encouraging. "But I, uh, don't think I have enough money on me to afford something like that –"

Again, the man waved his hand and gave a harsh laugh. "Now, now, I've been here for some time, and I've made it a point of pride to never offer something to someone that they can't afford. Being a parent at your age must be taxing enough, so I don't mind letting this go for a token amount. Deal?"

I took out a few bills and placed them on the counter, not able to suppress a smile forming from the man's kindly nature. "I still feel bad, but if you really don't mind – wait did you say parent?"

The man walked over and patted me on the shoulder, a blissful smile never leaving his face. "It's alright, there's no need to be embarrassed. Taking your whole family out like this is a wonderful thing, so there's no need to waste the rest of your evening with a tired old man like me. Go on now, go."

Before I could properly amend his misunderstanding, I was ushered out of the store, with Nina following not far behind.

"Master, what were you and that old man talking about for so long?" She gave me a quizzical look as Luna tried to give the man some parting words, though all she could manage was a half-yawned "Not a…child…" before falling back asleep.

"Ah, that – here." I opened my palm and offered the bell to Nina, who took it carefully, as if the slightest wrong move would shatter the whole thing. "It's for you, a little memento from our time together today. I thought it'd look nice on you."

Nina gasped and threw her arms around my neck, nuzzling her face against my chest. "Thank you thank you thank you master! This is the absolute bestest gift ever!"

I laughed and tried to pet her head gently with a free elbow. "I'm glad you like it. Now what do you say we head back home and get to work on dinner together? Lily should be getting back soon, and I'm sure Athena is wondering where we wandered off to." Nina happily nodded and grabbed onto my arm once more, the three of us setting off away from the urban horizon and towards the comfort of a familiar abode.

At least, that's what I thought.

After only a few minutes of walking, Nina suddenly jerked upright, like a current had shot through her body. I leaned down to ask what was wrong, but she only put a finger to her lips and craned her neck to the side, her ear twitching slightly.

"Master, do you hear it?"

I shook my head, befuddled. "Hear what?"

Nina's tail swayed carefully from side to side, as she leaned in towards this imperceptible sound.

"Something really loud came from over there." She pointed to her right, past a tightly packed row of buildings.

I shrugged, trying to push away a growing sense of unease. "Maybe it was a car crash or something? If it was far enough away that I couldn't hear it myself, we probably don't have much to worry about."

"Master..."

Without another word, I knew where this was going.

"Yeah...I know, you're right. Let's check it out. We should at least make sure no one is hurt."

Nina gave a strained smile and timidly grasped my hand in hers.

It didn't take long for our journey to be interrupted once more – what sounded like an enormous explosion boomed from what couldn't be more than several meters ahead of us.

In a moment, I was taken back to that day with Lily. We had heard a sound just like that back then, too. We went out to investigate, and met that monster...Why did this all feel so familiar? The explosion, the quiet, the next one –

Next one.

Without thinking, I grabbed Nina's side and pushed her behind me, throwing up one of my arms against my face. As

Nina fell to the ground, the wall in front of us burst into a hurricane of debris, throwing pieces of brick and wood against us. Although I made a poor shield, I seemed to have been able to take most of the impact, though it took everything I had not to get blown back on top of her. My entire body was engulfed in a burning ache, and my vision blurred through hazy waves of what used to be a set of buildings.

"M-s-r!"

I could vaguely hear someone shouting from behind me. Their voice was muffled, far too distant.

"W- h-e to g-!"

They tried to call out again, but all I could focus on was not stumbling to the ground. Even in this delirious state something kept telling me that if I fell down, it was all over. I had to do everything I could just…to…stay…up…

With a sudden jerk on my collar I was pulled back and to the ground. Nina was looking down at me with a fear I had never seen before – although my mind was still slow to catch up, the sight of her was enough to start bringing me back to reality.

"Master, are you ok?" Tears were welling up in her eyes – I wanted to reach out to comfort her, but my movements felt sluggish, as if my body couldn't keep up with what my mind was pushing me to do.

"I'm…I'm fine, thanks." I noticed that Luna was no long on my back and felt an instant of dread crawl over me, before seeing to my relief that she was leaning against Nina. "Do you…do you know what happened?"

Before she had a chance to respond, a new voice greeted me from where a store front had been just a moment ago.

"My, my – I sure know how to make an entrance, hmm?" The voice carried a youthful sort of haughtiness to it, accentuated by the sing-song manner of its delivery.

As I tried to peer through the ruinous fog, two figures at last emerged – one bulky, huge, and only in theory resembling a human, and the other a tall, slender, well-dressed man. I could feel Nina's grip on my shoulder tighten as she heard the person on the right speak again.

"I would ask you to hand over the girl to prevent any more harm coming to you or yours," the man said while lazily shuffling a deck of cards from one hand to the other, "but it appears luck would not be so forgiving today."

As I started to push myself off the ground, I was finally able to register what exactly I was seeing. The massive…thing on the left was certainly no human. It stood well over 8 feet tall, and appeared to be made entirely out of rock – differing shades of brown and grey were splashed across the creature's body, though its eyes (at least, based on where they were located I *assumed* they were eyes) shone a beaming red. For the time being it had stopped moving, standing perfectly still next to the man, who donned a vibrant outfit which, contrasted against his familiar's more muted features, made him stand out all the more. His jacket bore an array of shifting translucent colors, seemingly changing each time he shifted his pose, while his comparatively plain, black top hat was only garnished with a single violet affixed against the base. Something about this gaudy display felt all-too familiar…

"Hmph." The man crossed her arms and looked away in a huff. "The least you could do is show a little gratitude for such a grand display before you perish – it is the last you'll get to enjoy in this world, after all."

He seemed to cheer up at his own "joke" and gave a harsh laugh.

"I appreciate the gesture…" I had no idea who this was or what they were doing here, so my best option was to stall for time and figure it out as I went along. "But wouldn't it be common courtesy to at least introduce yourself first?"

"Master –" I felt Nina tug on my shirt as she whispered to me, but I could only squeeze her hand to try to reassure her that I knew what I was doing (regardless of the truth of the matter).

The man let out an exasperated sigh and threw one hand up. "I see no reason why you should care, but very well." With an exaggerated bow, he tipped his hat slightly towards me before giving a blank grin. "You have the honor of beholding Benjamin Cheret, the most talented – and efficient – mage in all the realms. Perhaps it is a shame that my audiences never have the pleasure of seeing a repeat performance, but then again –"

That empty smile returned.

"There's something to be said about a one-night-only special."

With his introduction finished, Cheret took a single card off the top of his deck and examined it aimlessly.

"To be perfectly honest, I don't know who you pissed off to get someone like me sent to your world." Cheret laughed to himself again, shaking his head. "My services don't come cheap, you understand? And with good reason – I never lea–"

"Wait!" I interjected, having no idea where I was going with this. But the longer I kept him talking, the more time I had to formulate something approaching a plan. "You're here to kill me, and you don't even know why?"

Cheret appeared shocked by the interruption, but quickly recovered his unnervingly calm and assured demeanor. "I know all that I need to know~"

He swapped his card with another from the deck and twisted it in his fingers – the otherwise entirely black back was overlaid with an ornate gold pattern, while the front contained an intricate and interwoven set of crimson symbols carefully etched into the material.

"Someone pays for my services, and I take care of their problem. What more reason do I need?" He smiled and shook his head once more, as if explaining something plainly obvious to a child.

"Well..."

C'mon, think, *think*.

"Wouldn't you at least do me the honor of granting a dying man's wish?"

Again, the man seemed somewhat taken aback. "And why would I care to do that?"

"Because you feel sorry for me?" I shrugged as I gently pushed Nina to my side, trying to create as much distance between the two of them as possible. "I mean after all, there's no way a simple human such as myself could stand up to the likes of you, so I was hoping–"

"You've got that right."

Before I could utter another sound, he flicked his wrist as a series of cards flew straight at us with near-imperceptible speed. Without thinking, I threw my body over Nina, feeling each finely honed edge dig into my back, a searing pain coursing throughout.

"Nina, take Luna home and find Athena. She'll know what to d–ARGH."

The burning sensation returned as I felt each card wrench itself out.

"But master –" Nina was shaking, nearly petrified with fear.

Even if I had no idea what I was doing, I had to stay brave. For her. For all of us.

"I'm fine, see?" I forced a smile through the pain and gave her a light pat on the head. "Just find Athena and bring her back here, ok?"

Nina wiped her eyes and gave a firm nod, lightly loading Luna onto her back as she took off with astounding speed, effortlessly bounding down the street in several wide leaps.

Cheret let out a sigh. "You know, I truly had no desire to make this any more drawn out than it needed to be. I suppose I'll just have to take care of the brat later." He had several cards fanned out in front of him, crimson blotches dripping from the edges. "Still, I see you have a little fight in you – commendable, perhaps, though the final result remains the same. Though this way is a bit…" He waved his hand around, flinging droplets of blood around him in a macabre shower. "*Messier*."

My attention was drawn back to Cheret's companion – the rock creature had been standing by his side, unmoving, during our entire exchange. However, just as he finished speaking, the monster began to lumber forward, each step deliberate, almost mechanical in its execution, as the mismatched pieces of stone shifted and ground against each other, leaving a faint trail of dust in its wake.

Taking a deep breath, I drew out my own weapon and tried to steady my thoughts, the feeling of the cracked leather hilt against my palm a strange source of comfort. Based on his initial attack, it seemed like Cheret might be more adept at fighting from a distance, while this creature was likely much slower, though powerful. If I could somehow slip past his companion, I could try to even the playing field a bit by fighting Cheret up-close – at least, that was my hope.

As I took a step back and prepared to make my move, the creature cast its shadow directly over me. I tried to hop to the side to preempt its attack, but it moved with startling alacrity – as I shifted to the right, a massive fist rushed into my side, sending me sprawling to the ground several feet away.

Wheezing, and digging my hands into the pavement as I struggled to my feet, I had no more than a half a second to register that another volley of cards were coming my way. I threw myself back down as they cut the air overhead, and tried to kick back off the ground to launch myself towards Cheret, but the creature blocked my path once more, a granite palm stopping my forward momentum abruptly.

My initial plan was already falling apart – despite the creature's massive size and rigid movements, it could attack with an unexpected speed. And if I tried simply running away, well...I'm sure Cheret would put an end to that attempt even quicker, as the continued throbbing along my back could attest to.

Finding my remaining options dwindling, I settled on an aggressive stall – if I went on the attack, I might be able to force an opening to escape. And inexperienced though I might be, this wasn't the first time I'd stared down a creature like this. With the benefit of Athena's training, I might even stand chance. Clinging to this nascent confidence, I leapt forward at the creature, my grip tightening as I approached and –

CRASH

Swiftly putting a foot down, I stopped my momentum mid-leap and pivoted past the creature's giant fist as it came down in front of me. With this momentary opening, I steadied my blade forward and aimed straight for Cheret's center, charging ahead with a reckless fervor known only to the desperate.

Reverberations shot through my arms as the weapon crashed ineffectively just a short distance from its intended target. Cheret let slip a barely-stifled laugh as the creature brought both fists rushing down towards me, which I narrowly avoided with a stumble backwards – in my place was left a small crater ringed by asphalt. Trying to scramble back to my feet, I felt an immense weight press against my chest, as the creature placed a hand on top of me.

"Tsk, tsk, tsk." Cheret clicked his tongue as he stepped forward and knelt down beside me. "I tried to warn you, did I not? Though I'll admit, I held some hope you might provide a bit more entertainment than this." He held up a single card and wiped it against his jacket. "All's the same in the end, I suppose."

And then, despite myself, I laughed. I laughed hard, and I laughed sincerely.

Cheret looked nonplussed, unable to process my sudden reaction.

"Y'know," I said as I shifted on my back, trying to wrestle free a full breath. "I can't die, right? Sure, you can do whatever you want to me, but it won't mean anything." I dropped my head back onto the pavement. "And by the time my friends get here, you'll have a lot more to worry about than just some weak human like me."

"Oh, my dear boy..." Cheret spoke with what could almost be mistaken for a measure of sympathy. "You think those pathetic bonds will help you?" The card he had been holding began to glow unnaturally, its luminescence almost hypnotizing. "Magic – the one thing that can break a contract, even with death."

I felt a chill pass over my heart.

"What are you talking about?"

Cheret smiled pleasantly. "Oh? And where could that flagrant confidence have scurried off to so soon?" He let out another cackle and slapped my cheek gently. "I know all about those spirits you've bound to this world – quite the feat for such an unassuming mortal, though such gifts amount to nothing more than parlor tricks when confronted with *true* power."

If he already knew about Lily and the others, then Whitehearst must too...and that meant it wasn't just me or Nina he was interested in. It was all of us.

I tried to push myself up, but the creature's hand only pressed down harder. I looked for my sword, for anything to use to fight back with, but it was no use – the weapon had scattered out of reach when I fell. Even if I could somehow grab it, I doubt I'd be given that much time to act in the first place.

As my soul processed what my mind could not, my thoughts returned to the girls I'd become so close to in such a short time. What would happen to them after this? Where would they go? They already felt like family to me, with all the happiness and frustrations that brought. And yet here I was, powerless to do anything to help myself, let alone them.

I closed my eyes as a renewed burning sensation burrowed through my chest, reaching lower and lower until I could feel my heartbeat slow with each labored breath.

Three beats.

Everything I had worked for, everything my friends had invested in me, all of it would mean nothing if I gave up here. But what could I do?

Two beats.

My vision started to blur and then fade as the pain sunk lower again. Was this really it?

One beat.

I said a silent apology to the girls who placed so much trust in me, and hoped that they understood that I tried.

I tried.

21

And then, it stopped.

I cautiously opened one eye – the creature was still crouched over top of me, stoic as ever. Turning my head to the side, however, I could see that Cheret was no longer there. Gingerly, I tried to sit up, and found that I wasn't met with any resistance. Scanning my surroundings, I was relieved to find Athena standing just a short distance down the road, with Lily and Nina not far off.

"Why would a mage go to such lengths over a single creature?" I overheard her ask. Since I seemed to be catching the middle of their conversation, I must have passed out for a few moments from the pain – her timing was impeccable in that regard.

"Wouldn't know, and even if I did, wouldn't care," Cheret said with a dismissive chuckle. "I do the job that's asked of me – no more, no less. You of all people should know how these things go, of course. Or need I remind you –?"

"*Silence.*" Athena spoke with a fierce hostility I had never heard from her before.

"Where's Yuu?" Lily interjected. Her voice was sharp, as if stifling a cry.

With a quick shove I was able to sit up, sending waves of agony coursing through my body. It seemed the previous scuffle had already taken its toll on me, but I had to keep moving, especially since the creature appeared to be docile for now (though how long that'd last, I couldn't be sure). Using one of its rocky arms to pull myself to my feet, I began to stagger towards the others.

A spark of recognition and relief lit across Lily's face, but I quickly held a finger to my lips. With a slight nod she returned her attention to Cheret, who must not have picked up on our silent exchange.

"My...*friend* has him rather preoccupied at the moment, don't you see?" Cheret gestured back, his fingers unfurling theatrically to match his melodramatic movements. "It'd be rude to interrupt the two while they're bonding like this, so whatever inquiries you have must be directed at yours truly, I'm afraid."

"If you hurt him..." Lily spoke barely above a whisper, but with an intensity that carried more impact than any scream could hope to match. Athena placed a hand on Lily's shoulder, which caused her body to relax somewhat, though the malevolence in her eye lost none of its furor.

"I have nothing against your *boyfriend*," he said with mock enthusiasm, "but I have a job, and it must be carried out. There is no reason to spill more blood here today, so if you'll hand over the girl, I'll be on my way."

Athena narrowed her eyes as she watched Cheret. "If we were to, you would leave Yuu unharmed, correct?" Nina gasped and was about to speak out in protest, but Lily squeezed her hand and shook her head quickly.

"I am nothing if not a man of my word." He beckoned at Nina. "So now – the creature, if you will."

Sensing this was my chance, I picked up my sword from the

ground and continued advancing towards the group.

"Hold." Athena held an arm out in front of Nina. "How can we be assured you will truly leave us be?"

Just a few more steps.

"I'll make this easy – " Cheret rolled his head from one side to the other. "You give me the girl and trust what I say. Or you don't – " He withdrew his deck of cards and dropped them from one hand to the other. "And not one of you leaves here alive."

At last, I was in range – I put all my weight onto my back foot and, pushing the overwhelming pain running through my body out of mind, leapt towards Cheret, blade once more aimed at his center. As I landed, I could feel the sickly slick sensation of steel driven through flesh as the sword finally found its mark, easily sliding through the mage's abdomen.

For a moment, all was silent.

Then, Cheret began to laugh.

His cackling soon degraded into howls of pain as he swiftly turned around to deliver a hard punch to my cheek. The blow stung, but I was able to maintain my balance and stay on my feet. In this brief time, however, the creature seemed to have reawakened, as it took only two wide steps torward me before bringing its fist down. I instinctually threw up my arms over my face to try to brace for it when –

"MASTE–" Nina's cry came close and was cut short in no more than instant. As I looked down, I could only see her body lying there – motionless – in the road.

No...No...Not like this.

I dropped to my knees, the entirety of the city having gone silent.

It can't be.

I grabbed Nina's arm, which laid limp in my hand. Her fingers uncurled, and a small, rusty golden bell fell on to the ground with a deafening crash.

She can't be.

I tried to move my body again, tried to pull her away, but all I could do was kneel and stare at the girl before me.

What is most important to you?

Who is most important to you?

For some reason, Luna's words rang through my head once more as the creature swung a massive fist into my side. I could feel the bones in my arm splinter and break, though there was no pain. Even as I was tossed onto the unforgiving sidewalk in a heap, I could only think of the girl lying so close, but still out of reach. Mustering all my will, I threw one arm out and dragged myself towards her, scraping my body against the rough cement. Far away, I could vaguely hear Lily call out, though her words were muffled and distorted.

Using the last of my energy, I tried to pull myself a little closer – if I could just reach Nina, she would be fine. She would wake up, we could put this behind us, we could all go home together. The smoldering remnants of sunlight cast long shadows across our bodies, as someone – or something – stood over us.

With a cold resignation creeping over me, I cast my gaze up to see Lily, tears streaming down her cheeks. Without a word, she dropped down and hugged my face close to her waist. Unable to speak or move, I closed my eyes and let the encroaching darkness overtake my senses.

* * *

Slowly, drearily, I came to. My memories of what happened

earlier in the day were still jumbled; I could recall going out with Nina and Luna, and making our way home, and then–

My chest tightened as a cruel realization was reignited inside me. I sat up with a jolt, causing the room to start swaying and nausea to overtake me.

"It's ok, it's ok." A soft, gentle voice greeted me, as I felt an icy hand push my head back down slowly. "You can't get up so quickly, so just try to rest for now."

Turning to my side, I saw Lily sitting next to the bed, her furrowed brow softened by a relieved smile.

"Is...Does..." I wasn't sure how to ask the question I dreaded getting an answer to. "Where's Nina?"

Lily smiled with some amusement and pointed behind me – sure enough, Nina was lying next to me, curled up in a ball, her quiet breathing indicating that she was sound asleep. Just as quickly as my fears had arisen, they were dispersed. I patted her head lightly, not wanting to disturb her, and turned my attention back to Lily.

"Do...do you know what happened?"

"A little...as soon as that man attacked you, Athena stepped in. She was able to strike him with her sword..." Lily shivered at the memory, clearly uncomfortable with the image it left. "But he seemed to have gotten away. When I saw you lying there on the ground though, I, I–"

Lily's voice was strained, so I wrapped my hand around hers, our fingers intertwined. Despite her cold touch, I could feel my face start to warm as my skin pressed so intimately against hers.

"I'm just glad you're ok," she said with a small laugh. "We were just as worried about Nina, too, but thankfully she was only out for a little bit. She kept asking about you the entire time we were carrying the two of you home." Lily smiled pitifully, shaking her head.

I wasn't sure what to say; wasn't sure what I *could* say. Time after time these girls had saved my life, and now at no small cost to their own well-being.

"Lily?"

"Hm?" She looked at me curiously.

"Thank you. Really." She blushed lightly and turned her head away, so her hair was covering most of her face.

"You don't have to thank me…" she mumbled quietly.

I squeezed her hand, understanding what she truly meant.

"By the way, do you know where Athena is now?"

Lily jolted up, as if she just remembered something important. "Oh! Yes –" Looking towards the door, she called out. "You can come in now~"

Light streamed in from the hallway, an artificial spotlight cast on the three of us, as Athena shuffled in with unusual timidity.

"Hello, Yuu. How are you feeling?"

"Eh, no worse for wear all things considered."

I tried to wave her over, but realized that my arm had been set with a makeshift sling, the familiarly rough handiwork suggesting it was Lily's doing. Through our various misadventures I had come to find that even my more serious injuries would heal on their own given enough time, so a broken arm was nothing much to stress over.

"As ill-minded as I know it to be, I must still commend you for your fortitude earlier. What you did was brash, dangerous, illogical, reckless, uncertain, and –" Athena sighed, and sat down next to Lily. "You must swear to never do something like that again, am I clear?"

"I–" I wanted to protest, but cut myself off. "Alright, I'll be more careful next time. I'm sorry for putting you and everyone else in danger."

Athena shook her head and offered a sympathetic smile. "I would hardly expect a novice such as yourself to handle the situation with any more finesse than you did. I am afraid, however, that if the danger Whitehearst poses to you was not clear before, it must be precisely evident now."

"Yeah, about that..." Athena leaned forward, resting her chin on her hands as I spoke. "Why does he care so much about Nina? I mean, couldn't he just find someone else like her?"

Athena shifted uncomfortably, searching for words that, for one reason or another, would not come easy. "Although I will admit to possessing very little knowledge of the man himself, his actions betray a certain...way of being."

"How do you mean?"

"Men like that do not take kindly to transgressions of any sort. I would cast my doubt that he truly cares for the situation you or Nina have placed him in at present; rather, it is a matter of pride. He will not be satisfied until he feels that he has reasserted his authority, and reaffirmed his place in the hierarchy of his own design."

"He'd go that far out of his way to get Nina back, and he doesn't even care about what happens to her? She was already hurt–" A new thought came to me. "And what happened to that rock creature? I know Lily said you took care of the mage, but she didn't mention the monster at all."

Lily looked away and laughed nervously, while Athena let out an exasperated sigh.

"When that man escaped, he left his familiar behind. I thought to fully pacify it, but as it appeared docile, Lily insisted that we spare it for the present time – she suggested you would feel the same."

"Well, I mean – she's not wrong. If it was only acting on its master's orders, then there's no reason for us to hurt it. But even then, there's no telling how dangerous it still is...Where's it at now?"

"In the backyard!" Lily answered cheerfully.

"As in...our backyard? Here?"

"Yup!" She smiled to herself, satisfied.

"The creature followed us home, despite our efforts to the contrary," Athena explained. "It has not moved from its spot since arriving here."

I threw my head back onto the pillow and covered my face with my hand. "Please tell me the neighbors haven't noticed... " I muttered to no one in particular. "Hey, Lily – do you still have Mae's phone number?"

She nodded, giving me a curious look. "Do you need something from her?"

"Maybe it's a stretch, but if anyone can help us with that thing outside, I figure it's her."

Lily happily agreed and passed me her phone (for sake of convenience, I had bought each of the girls a cellphone a few weeks earlier, though Lily seemed to be the only one to use it with some regularity).

A few button presses later, and the sound of an airy, slightly timid, voice filled my ear. "Hello? Lily? Is everything ok?"

"Heya, actually it's Yuu. I'm borrowing her phone for just a bit. I have a bit of a favor to ask if you don't mind."

"Oh...oh! O-of course, what do you need?"

"It might be easier to explain if you just come over and see for yourself, honestly. Do you still have that book with you too?"

"The one I showed you last week? Hmm..." Mae went quiet as she thought for a moment. "I do! I took it home with me after, uh, all the things we talked about, heh...heh." She gave an awkward laugh as her plain embarrassment emanated through the phone. I guess she still hadn't forgotten what happened during our first club meeting.

"If you don't mind, could you bring that with you? I'll tell you more when you get here."

After giving her my address, I hung up and turned back to Lily and Athena.

"Well, she's on her way, so hopefully she'll know more than we do."

"She?" Athena asked.

"Oh, yeah – a friend of mine and Lily's. We joined her club at school, and she seems to know a bit about otherworldly things, so..." I shrugged. "Here's hoping."

"A human who is aware of the other realms...fascinating." Athena seemed to be lost in thought as she stared off to the side, tapping her chin. "That being that, I will return to the first floor and check once more upon the creature's condition. It would be ill-fated if it were to escape while we were otherwise preoccupied."

I thanked Athena as she left, and decided it would be best to get cleaned up while I had the chance. After a brief, if somewhat uncomfortable, shower (given my current condition, trying to move around only incited more pain), and throwing on a fresh change of clothes, I headed downstairs to meet Mae outside.

Mae was standing just beside the worn wooden gate, a plain auburn jacket wrapped tightly around her body and a tattered leather book nestled under her arm. I waved to her as I approached, leaving the door open for her to enter.

"Hey, thanks for coming over on such short notice. The thing I wanna show you is in the backyard."

"I-it's no problem," Mae stammered, following me into the house. "But, um...what happened to your arm?"

"Oh, this?" I wriggled my other arm and shook my head. "I think you'll figure it out once I show y– "

"Hi Mae!" Lily called out as she saw her walk into the living room. "How have you been?"

"Oh, hi Lily. I-I've been ok. Are you still coming to the club this week?"

"Of course! Both of us will." Lily smiled warmly, which Mae meekly returned.

Just then I heard a door close, as Athena stepped into the room as well. "Ah, you must be Yuu's friend from school. It's a pleasure to finally meet you." Athena gave a small curtsy as Mae looked from Lily, to me, to Athena, and back to me again.

"There's more...?" she asked in disbelief.

"Uh, yeah, I guess," I replied somewhat awkwardly. "It's kind of a long story."

I could see a flicker of intensity flash across Mae's eyes, but she took a deep breath and seemed to calm herself.

"Alright, well – there's something you wanted to show me in particular?"

"Mhm, right over here." I led Mae to the backyard, with Lily and Athena following shortly behind.

The creature stood completely still, the tiniest sign of life completely absent. If I hadn't known better, I would have thought it was just some crudely designed statue – which, given its actual makeup, maybe wasn't too far off.

"This...thing followed us home, and we're not really sure

what to do with it. I was hoping you might know what it is, and be able to tell us more...about...it?"

Mae wandered over to the creature as if in a trance, her book falling to the grass with a dull thud. She carefully traced the outline of one of the creature's jagged arms with her finger, scrutinizing the fine bumps and grooves of each granite ligament.

"It's real..." she muttered breathlessly. "It's really real. They exist." She turned back to me, a burning of passion barely contained in her eyes. "Where did you find him? Where did he come from? Do you know what this is?"

With each question, Mae had taken a step closer, forcing me to place my hand on her head and gently push her back.

"That's the problem – we don't have any idea what it is, or why it's here now. As for where it came from...How do I explain this..." I looked to Lily and Athena for help, but they were at a loss as to what to say as well. "Basically, some guy attacked us along with our rocky friend over here. But when he ran away, he left this behind, which followed us home. It seems, uh, nice enough for now, but I'm not sure it belongs here."

Mae seemed to have completed her inspection, nodding to herself as I finished speaking. She retrieved her book from the ground and began to swiftly flip through it, stopping abruptly at a certain page.

"Aha, I knew it! Look –" She grabbed my sleeve and pulled me to her side, holding the book open for me to see. Sure enough, in a roughly-hewn outline, was an illustration of a creature more or less the same as the one standing before us; although some of the finer details were different (the creature in the book was less bulky, for one), there was no mistaking the likeness.

"So…what is it?"

Mae sighed and pointed to a tiny scribble below the illustration that I now understood was supposed to be writing.

"It says right here."

"You're saying you can read that?"

"W-well, yeah, I wrote it after all…"

Oops.

"Oh, uh, I'm sorry, it's – it's just that since it's so dark out right now, it's a bit hard for me to see." If I were being honest, I don't think *any* amount of light would have let me decipher what was written there, but that was a fact better kept to myself. "So, what exactly does it say?"

"This creature is a golem…" Mae appeared to be transfixed by the page, intently reading through lines of varying style and organization, suggesting that the book had gone through many owners before reaching her. "They're beings made of inanimate material brought to life through magic, though their exact level of sentience tends to vary wildly." She glanced up and ran her hand along a smooth piece of rock that served as the creature's wrist. "Really, to even make one of this size must've taken an incredible amount of power and skill…"

That last part didn't exactly instill a lot of confidence in me, but I tried to stay focused on the matter at hand.

"Do you have any clue why it'd start following us around?"

Mae took a step back and looked the creature up and down, as if sizing it up. "It's just my hypothesis, but golems are only supposed to respond to the one who created them. If that person left, and without any further instructions, it'd probably just attach itself to the nearest person it could find."

"So you're saying it…imprinted on us?"

"Yeah, something like that," Mae said with a giggle.

"But then what should we do now? I don't think it's moved since it decided to settle in here, but we can't just leave it sitting out in the open all day."

Mae pulled the book closer to her face, carefully scanning across each individual note.

"The only thing it says here...is that when a golem has finished its task, or its creator so wishes, it will cease function and disintegrate. That's all assuming the creator is around, however; I'm not sure what'll happen now that that connection seems to be severed." She looked back up at the golem, then declared cheerfully, "Either way, it'll be interesting!"

"I'm glad at least one of us is enjoying the situation," I mumbled.

It was easy enough to pass the girls off as normal humans, just so long as they didn't do anything too strange. A giant rock monster was gonna be a lot harder to hide, but I couldn't just send it out on its own. And since it must've been controlled by Cheret, or even Whitehearst, then I couldn't even really blame it for hurting Nina. If anything, it deserved a chance to live as its own being.

"Alright!" Clapping my hand against my side, I approached the golem. "Since it seems like you have nowhere else to go, you're welcome to stay with us from now on. I'm not even sure if you can hear me right now, but...I hope you catch my drift either way." I stared at the creature's face for some time, waiting for any sign of recognition or response. However, after a few moments passed without so much as a subtle movement, I figured that was the end of it, and turned away, an odd feeling of dejection weighing on my heart.

Lily placed a chilly hand on my shoulder and smiled sympathetically. "If it makes you feel any better, I don't think anyone else would know what to do in this kind of situation. But the fact that you're willing to take care of him really shows the kind of person you are."

"Heh, I appreciate it. I just don't know what we should do now – I don't like leaving it out here all alone, but I'm not sure how we can get it to wake up or whatever. I don't even know what'll happen if it *does* wake up."

Athena stood by my other side, arms crossed, as she continued to fix her gaze on the creature. "Compassion tempered by prudence is indeed the wisest choice. I've no doubt in time we will come to understand the true nature of this creat–"

"Look!" Lily gasped as the sound of rock scraping against rock filled the air, the golem's joints grinding against each other as a soft, red glow returned to its eyes.

Before I could say another word, it reached out a wide hand and hovered it over me.

"Yuu–!" Athena cried out, but I held her arm as she reached for her sword, signaling her to wait.

Slowly, almost gingerly, the golem placed its hand on my shoulder, the same as Lily had done. With a combination of fear and anticipation, I tried to speak to it again.

"Can you understand me?"

A small pause. The piercing sound of shifting granite returned as the golem's head near-imperceptibly rose and fell in short order.

"Do you want to stay with us?"

Again, the same movement.

"I'm, uh, sorry, but I'm not sure you'll fit inside..." I glanced at the doorway, and then back at the creature – its height would prevent it from entering even the most generous of doors, and its overall size would stop it from going anywhere in the house (at least while keeping the floors and walls intact).

The golem now turned its head from left to right, and moved its hand to the side, as if gesturing towards the ground.

"You're ok out here?"

Another nod.

I turned to the others, a half smile on my face. "I guess if it's ok with you all, I think we have a new member of the household."

Lily hugged Mae excitedly, while Athena offered her own terse approval.

"Then, uh…welcome to your new home."

The golem gave one final affirmation, before sitting down in a corner between the fence and the house, the red glow in its eyes fading to a dull crimson.

"I'm not sure what to say, Mae, other than thank you." I glanced back at the golem as I followed Lily and Athena inside, the top of its head sitting just below the fence. "We still have to figure out how to keep him better hidden, but – well, you've been a huge help, especially on such short notice. So if there's anything I can do to return the favor, just let me know."

Mae shook her head quickly. "No no, you've already given me all that I could've hoped for and so much more!" She stopped suddenly as a new idea came to her. "Although, um, if it's not too much, there…there is one way you can thank me."

"Sure, if it's something I can do."

"If…if you find any more creatures or things from other worlds like this, will you let me know? I promise I'll keep it a secret! It's just…I've never had a chance to see them in person like this before. It's – " She took a deep breath, calming her nerves. "It's really amazing."

"Of course – that'd be an even bigger help for us, honest. None of us seem to know much about these kinds of creatures, so any expertise you can give us would be great."

With an excited and overall satisfied smile, Mae gave a quick nod and hurried off soon after we all exchanged our good-byes. Although I was happy to so quickly turn a one-time enemy to friend (or the next closest thing to it), deep inside I knew that the storm clouds gathering on the horizon were closer than ever.

22

"Coming, coming."

As the quick rapping on the door continued unabated, I got up from the couch to go see who it was. I had been spending the day relaxing with Lily and watching her favorite series on tv, trying to shake the image of Nina's still body from my mind. For her part, she seemed no worse for wear in the morning, filling the house with excited chattering about this, that and anything. And so while I tried to hide it – for her sake as much as everyone else's – those feelings of fear and resentment towards my own ineptitude continued to roil deep inside.

"Hi, how can I help you?" I asked as I opened the door.

"Hey kid, long time no see. Mind if I talk to you for a bit?" Standing in front of me was a tall man in a slightly disheveled suit, his tired eyes a clear indication of his identity.

"Oh, hey Rick. Uh, sure, come on in."

I opened the door for the enigmatic agent and moved to the kitchen to start filling the kettle with water.

"Can I get you something to drink? Coffee, tea?"

"That's very kind of you – coffee's fine."

For a while, neither of us spoke, with only the sound of the stove grumbling as it warmed up to fill the stale silence.

"So, I see you've been busy," Rick said at last. "And I guess you already know that keeps *me* busy as well."

I laughed nervously, not sure what his intention was. "Ah, yeah, I…I'm sorry about that."

An awkward quiet overtook us once more.

As soon as kettle began to whistle, I jumped up to turn off the burner and began to pour water into two cups.

"You don't trust me, do you?" Rick asked suddenly.

I set the kettle back on the stove and gave it some serious thought. I guess I really didn't – for one reason or another, I always felt a sense of apprehension when seeing him, though I could never exactly put my finger on why. He had been friendly enough to me and Lily, and he hadn't come after us even as we took in more spirits, but there was still something that bothered me…

"What exactly is it that you do?" I asked in return.

"I told you before, didn't I? I know it's been a while, but–"

"No, no – I mean what is it you *really* do?"

I sat down across from Rick as he eyed me curiously. A thin tension began to build, before being broken sharply by a hearty laugh – the first I'd ever heard from the man.

"Alright, alright, I suppose there's no reason to keep it from you any longer. You can tell your friends they don't have to hide over there, either."

Puzzled, I turned around in my seat to see three girls walk out from behind the wall.

"We didn't mean to eavesdrop…" Lily said softly.

"I was only doing my due diligence in watching over my student," Athena protested.

"Sorry master…" Nina finished sheepishly.

"It's no problem, I'm just wondering – wait." I looked back at Rick. "How'd you know they were all there?"

Chuckling to himself, he looked up and to his side. "You can come out now, too."

Without a moment's delay, a slender woman in glasses materialized by Rick's side. She was dressed in a white button-up with a simple black vest, which projected an aura of clean professionalism that stood in stark contrast to Rick's more disheveled facsimile.

"Hello everyone," the woman said at last. "It's a pleasure to finally make your acquaintance."

"Uh, hi there," I said, the pieces slowly starting to fall into place. "I don't mean to be rude, but – "

"Master," Nina said urgently as she tugged on my sleeve. "That's a–"

"Spirit, yes," Rick finished for her. "I'd like you all to meet my faithful companion, Morgan."

The woman gave a slight bow, offering a warm and earnest smile. "I'm sorry I never had a chance to show myself to you before." She glanced at Rick, her smile fading somewhat. "You see…there's a reason he took so much interest in you before. It's highly unusual for spirits to bind themselves to humans, and even less so without drawing the attention of the PL."

"PL?" I asked.

"Project Leviathan," Rick clarified. "It's the organization I've been working with for the past several years."

"Why would they care if humans and spirits were interacting, though?"

Rick and Morgan looked at each cautiously, before the former spoke up again.

"To put it simply, they have an…interest in why spirits and the like have been showing up in our world all of a sudden. They've done their best to keep it out of the public eye to avoid potential unrest, but things go a bit deeper than that."

"Then what is their goal?" Lily ventured.

Again, Rick seemed burdened by what was to come. After a brief silence, Morgan spoke up.

"Do you know of the Leviathan?"

"It's a kind of mythical sea creature, right?" I said.

"In a sense, yes." Morgan paused, tapping her fingers along the back of Rick's chair. "However, to the PL, it is something much more. Though the evidence is scant, they believe it to be the key to understanding how this and every other world is connected. And so to accomplish this, they have been tasked with taking charge of those beings not native to this world – though what they do after apprehending such creatures and spirits remains inscrutable at present. It's an…unfortunate situation, to say the least."

"Wait, wait – but if the people you work for want you to capture spirits, how are you still bound to one?"

Rick closed his eyes and rubbed his temples. "I won't lie, it hasn't been easy. We've had some close calls over the years, but thankfully the last place these people would think to look is within their own ranks. With a little prudence and some plausible deniability, no one tends to bat an eye at the things I know – or pretend to."

"What are you talking about?"

Rick smirked and nodded towards Lily and Athena, who were standing behind me.

"I don't think I need to tell you what happens when you enter into a contract with a spirit, do I?"

"I…guess not, but I'm still not sure I follow. Why would you agree to contract with a spirit when your whole job is trying to track them down? I mean, you said it's been years, so if you were just trying to turn on her, I don't think she'd still be around."

Rick gave a dejected sigh as Morgan giggled and placed a hand on his shoulder.

"C'mon kid, give me a little credit." He stared down at his mug as his voice grew quieter. "I was young and stupid. I dunno, maybe I still am. I'd heard about all these unexplainable events going on, kept seeing the damage that was done in their wake. It was due to 'outside forces', I remember some nameless suit telling me when I first started working for the city. When a position opened up, I was all too eager to join – but it was only after meeting her that I started to understand the truth."

Morgan nodded to herself, a satisfied smile not leaving her lips.

"When I first entered your realm, I had no idea where I was or what had happened. Rick had been looking into some creature that had wandered into this world around the same time, and so that's when I stumbled upon him – or rather, he upon me."

"I thought she was the source of our problems at first." Rick shook his head. "It was the first time I'd ever met something – or someone – from another world. I actually didn't believe her at first, given how she looks just like any other human."

Lily and I glanced at each other – a familiarity we shared.

"After she explained what was going on, I didn't have the heart to turn her in. And so it was there, in the middle of my investigation, that I made a pact with her."

"He offered me his protection," Morgan said wistfully.

"And she lent me her ability to locate spirits and the like. It comes in handy when trying to limit the destruction done by some of the more malevolent, or at least beastly, ones." He smirked as he stared down into his mug. "Though seems you've managed to beat us to the punch a few times already."

"Trouble does seem to have its way of finding me..." I decided not to finish with the "despite my best efforts" running through my mind. "Anyway, I'm guessing you didn't come all the way here just to tell me that, did you?"

"No, no – I'll get straight to the point" Rick clasped his hands together, now looking at me intently. "Another otherworldly creature showed up yesterday, somewhere around 2nd street. That's where that little bistro is – you know the one?"

I nodded carefully. "I do."

"Great. Now what I saw there yesterday was...unusual, to say the least."

I felt I knew where this was going, but I had to ask regardless. "How do you mean?"

"When destructive creatures find themselves in this world, the damage they cause tends to be random – some broken walls, some shattered windows, that sort of thing. It's usually easy to play off as just some vandalism, and people tend to believe it because that's the most reasonable explanation. Now, to them, it might look like more of the same – maybe damages were on the heavier side, but saying a gas line exploded seemed to do the trick."

"I...still don't understand what that has to do with me."

Rick held up his hand. "Hold on – I'm getting there. The damage in that area didn't seem random to me; in fact, it looked like there was a fight." I forced myself to meet Rick's gaze directly as he continued. "Someone's after you, right? I don't know who, I don't know why, but it's simple enough to figure out that someone has it out for you."

I looked to Lily, Athena, and Nina in turn, but they seemed just as uncertain with how to proceed as I was. Taking a deep breath, I made my decision.

"Yes, me and Nina were attacked yesterday." I put my hand on Nina's head to signify who I was talking about, since I didn't have the chance to formally introduce her yet. "We helped rescued her from a man named Gregory Whitehearst about a month or two ago. I don't know much about him, other than that he's a mage, he can enter this world, and now he has a vendetta against us – or, uh, me in particular, I suppose."

Pausing briefly, I considered what needed to be said next.

"I'm sorry I didn't trust you before. I guess I just wasn't sure why you'd taken such an interest in all of us here."

Rick let out a genuine laugh and leaned back in his chair. "No hard feelings, kid. I suppose I gave you enough reason to feel that way, what with keeping all of this from you. I didn't want to get you wrapped up in all the politicking if I could avoid it, but now it seems I have to be a little more forward in my efforts."

"What is it that you are implying?" Athena asked cautiously.

"I know less about mages than I do spirits and creatures, them being a secretive lot and all, but there is one thing I have no doubt about – whoever this man is, he's a threat. Not just to you, but lots of other people who don't even have the slightest clue these other worlds exist."

"We have already ascertained that," Athena said tersely. As she spoke, her gaze was fixed on my arm still resting in a sling – I guess I wasn't the only one still dwelling on the previous day's events.

"Great! Then you already know you'll need all the allies you can get, I'm sure."

"You want to help us?" I asked.

"Of course, of course – I am a public servant and all that.

Even if it's not a direct order, I can still work to serve the common good."

Morgan, who had been oddly quiet for some time, started to shift nervously. Even if I had little choice but to trust Rick, I knew he was still holding back something important.

"And what's in it for you?"

"Ah! I hoped we'd get to that – I figure if we help each other, we can still further our own individual goals. Then it's a win-win, right?"

"I…guess that makes sense."

Rick's jovial tone dissipated just as quickly as it had appeared. "Whether you've realized it or not, you have a substantial amount of power available to you. Not just in the gifts given to you – in the friends you have right now, too." He looked up at Morgan and gave a weak smile before returning his attention to me. "You want to protect these girls, right?"

"Of course."

"And how far would you be willing to go for them?"

"I'd do whatever it takes."

"Even if it cost you your life?"

"No question."

"Yuu–!"

"You couldn't–!"

"Master–!"

All three girls spoke at once, to which Rick only laughed and shook his head in amusement.

"You're quite the lucky fellow, you know that? But don't worry – if we work together, there's no reason it should come to that. All I'm asking is that you're ready to help me in return when the time comes."

"But what kind of 'help' are you looking for?"

Morgan stepped forward this time, a pleading look in her eyes.

"Something is going on with the PL...We don't know what it is exactly, but they've redoubled their efforts as of late, and seem to be even more intent on capturing beings from other worlds – especially spirits."

"It's all very hush-hush, as you'd imagine," Rick clarified. "Only those at the center of it all know what's really happening. I'll step up my own investigation in the meantime, but I may need your help when things get serious."

A dense silence broke between us, as we all considered the implications of what Rick was suggesting.

"I won't tell you that you have to do this, kid. On my word, I can walk out your door right now and pretend this conversation never happened. The final decision rests with you and your friends."

I paused, mulling it over.

"If we agree, you'll give us your protection, right?"

Rick stretched back, the slightest hint of a smile returning to his haggard countenance.

"Well, maybe not me exactly. But I have enough clout in the organization that I'm sure I can muster some guys to look over things for a while. If anything seems fishy, they'll check it out, and you'll be none the wiser. You can more or less go about your days without having to worry about some creep coming to get ya."

The proposition was enticing. When I first met Lily, I thought my biggest worry would be introducing her to this new world and trying to teach her about love. But as we met more spirits, fought more creatures, and became entwined with powers well beyond our understanding, those relatively peaceful days seemed to be slipping away. Naïve as it might be, I didn't want to lose that – I didn't want to live fearing for their safety, for what might happen at any moment. Even if this meant certain danger in the future, it was worth it to recapture that sense of normalcy for now.

"Then...I agree."

"Excellent!" Rick threw up his arms in a rare expression of enthusiasm.

"Wait –"

"Huh? Something the matter?"

"You said you needed not just me, but the girls here, too. I can't make the decision for all of them. What do you think?"

"You keep worrying so much about protecting and taking care of us, the least we can do is support you in return," Lily said warmly.

"Until that certain day comes to pass, I shall always accompany you on whatever such journey you choose to take," Athena added.

"Whatever master needs, Nina is here for him," Nina finished.

"Oh, and there's one more, but she's kind of always asleep, so she might have to sit this one ou–"

I was interrupted by a soft thud from behind. Turning around, I saw Luna lying on the floor, face-down. We rushed to get up and help her, but could only share a relieved laugh as she gave a weary thumbs-up and a muffled "Me too."

"Well, that seems to settle it," Rick said as I carried Luna into the kitchen and sat her on my lap. "If anyone gives you trouble, give me a call and I'll be sure to come by." He reached into his jacket pocket and produced a plain, white notecard, on which he quickly jotted down his phone number before handing it to me.

"Thanks, I'll keep that in mind."

Despite everything Rick had told us, I still felt conflicted about my decision. Was this really going to keep us all safe, or was I just sending us into even more danger than before? The thought weighed heavily on me as the two took their leave.

"It was very nice finally getting to meet all of you – I hope we can talk again on more pleasant circumstances sometime soon," Morgan said as she followed Rick out the door.

I turned to the rest of the girls, who were still standing behind me, as if waiting for something.

"Uh, now that that's finished, what should we do?"

"I could use some help in the garden should you be inclined to assist me in some manual labor," Athena said bluntly.

"I wouldn't mind spending some quality time on the couch… " Lily said shyly.

"Let's go an adventure!" Nina said bounding up and down next to me.

"Bed…" Luna mumbled, her head falling gently on my chest as she dozed off again.

I shook my head, smiling to myself – whatever the cost may be, this was worth protecting.

23

A few uneventful weeks passed by, and it seemed Rick was as good as his word, at least for the time being. All of us were able to achieve some semblance of peace, forgetting about the danger surrounding us for some time. And so it was on one of these relatively idyllic days that Lily suggested the five of us go out to dinner together, something we hadn't thought to do in quite a while.

"Sure, why not? We don't have too many chances to spend time all together like this, so it'd be a nice opportunity."

"Great! I'll tell the others and we'll get ready right away~" Lily hurried off towards the stairs, a happy aura lingering in her wake.

Figuring I should follow suit, I set to make my way upstairs as well, but bumped into Nina as I turned the corner.

"Um, master…" Nina mumbled.

"Hey there, everything ok?"

She gave a timid nod, but it was clear something was bothering her.

"Nina overheard Lily say we're going out together, right?"

"Mhm, that's what we were hoping at least. Are you not feeling well?"

I placed a hand on her forehead, but the only excessive heat seemed to be radiating from her cheeks.

"No, no! It's not that, it's just..." She looked out the glass door forlornly. "What about the monster outside? Won't he be lonely?"

It seemed obvious when Nina said it, but I had almost forgotten about our golem friend. I had tried several times to talk to it, but there was only so much conversation that could be had with only "yes" and "no" responses. It seemed to enjoy helping Athena tend to the garden at least, so I don't think it was bored, but maybe there was still something more we could do to reach out to it?

"I...don't think it can come with us, since it'd kind of stand out. I don't think it really eats, either. It doesn't have a mouth, right?" I looked back to Nina. "Does it?"

She shook her head swiftly, much to my relief.

"But can't we bring something home for him, please? Nina will find something good she swears!" Nina planted her feet firmly and pursed her lips in determination – just like Lily, as soon as she had set her mind to something, it was all she could think about.

"Alright, alright – that's a good idea. It's almost Christmas anyway, so we should do a little shopping while we're out."

Nina's eyes lit up at the mere mention of the word as she cooed with wonder.

"Master, what's that?"

"Christmas?" I paused, trying to think how best to explain it to someone who had never heard of it before. I wasn't particularly religious, so that angle didn't seem to make sense, but trying to describe the more general aspects might just confuse her. "Well, y'see –"

Thankfully, just at that moment Lily came back downstairs,

having changed into a dark purple dress and affixing a white flower behind her ear. It was a simple outfit, but I had to admit – she looked gorgeous.

"What's everyone talking about?" she asked as she approached us.

I guess I didn't notice how long I was staring, since her brow quickly furrowed with worry.

"Yuu? Is everything alright?"

"Oh, uh, yeah, everything's great. I just…" I had never felt this nervous around Lily before. Now for whatever reason my heart was racing, and I was stumbling over my words. Taking a deep breath, I decided to just be honest with her. "You look amazing, Lily. Really."

"Yuu…" Lily blushed and turned away, covering her face. "You shouldn't say things like that so suddenly, you'll make me–"

Before she could finish, Nina's high-pitched voice cut her off.

"Lily Lily Lily! Do you know what Christmas is? Yuu won't tell Nina." She glared at me, crossing her arms in a huff.

"I was going to tell you in just a second…" I tried to offer, but Nina either didn't hear or didn't care.

"Christmas, Christmas…" Lily tapped her lips thoughtfully, as if searching through a library of memories. "Oh! I know~" She moved herself to the couch, patting her lap for Nina to come sit on, to which the latter obliged. "Every Christmas, a benevolent and magical being named Santa visits the houses of all the good boys and all the good girls, leaving presents for them to wake up to in the morning. And – " Lily held a finger up as Nina stared at her, entranced. "If you write him a letter, he will grant whatever wish you send him."

"Any…?" Nina said slowly, leaning forward.

"Mhm! He must be one of the most powerful spirits in all the worlds, though fortunately he only uses his abilities for good. So be sure to be on your best behavior, and Santa will surely grant your wish." Lily touched Nina's nose playfully as she finished.

"Nina will, she will! She needs to write her letter right now so Santa gets it in time!" Without wasting another second, Nina bounded up the stairs and out of sight.

"You really know a lot about Christmas, huh?" I asked as I sat down next to Lily.

"Oh, no, not really…It's just, I knew someone special – a long time ago – that told me all about it." Lily gave a weak smile as she looked at me, something clearly weighing on her mind. "It always feels bittersweet when I think about it, but this is my first time celebrating it in this world. And even more importantly –" She rested her head on my shoulder and closed her eye. "With you."

Once more my heart began to race as I felt Lily's cool cheek press against me. Was she always this cute? I mean, sure, we already slept in the same bed, and she didn't seem to have many qualms about physical affection, but it felt like I was seeing her in a completely different light.

"I'm, uh, really happy I get to spend it with you too," I stammered. I knew I sounded like an idiot, not even being able to talk to the girl who was supposed to have been my girlfriend for the past several months. "I…don't want to pry, but who was this special person you were talking about?"

Out of the corner of my eye, I could see Lily's fingers tighten around the edges of her dress, then relax.

"Do you remember when we first met? How I said spirits like

me don't get usually get to spend much time around humans?"

"Yeah, my memory's a bit fuzzy, but I remember you mentioning something to that effect."

"That...wasn't entirely the truth, or at least –" She bit her lip, struggling to express what was locked in the most precious corners of her heart.

"It's alright, you don't have to tell me all at once if you – "

"No!" She turned to me, impassioned. That overwhelming sincerity and determination so uniquely hers pressed well upon me, so all I could do was nod and give her the time she needed. "It's not that, honest. It's just...you're not the first human I've grown close to."

For some reason, I felt my heart stop a moment as she said that. Was there someone else that she really cared for? I knew it was hypocritical to feel any sort of sadness if she did, but I couldn't deny the small twinge of jealousy that cut across me in that moment.

"Oh...where are they now?"

It was the only thing I could think to ask.

"They passed away some years ago," Lily said quietly. "I think that's why we became so close – he knew his time would be coming, and so I was drawn to him." She looked to me and gave a strained smile. "It didn't stay like that, though. The more we got to know each other, the more we cared for one another. He would tell me all of his favorite things to do, like reading stories of adventure, and crafting little boats out of scraps of wood. By the time I met him, he was already too sick to go outside much, so he always said his greatest escape was through his own mind..."

Lily trailed off, as memories of her departed friend must have come flooding back all at once. For a while, we both just sat in silence together.

"What was his name?"

"Grey…His name was Grey." This time, Lily smiled fondly, as if speaking her friend's name pushed away the melancholy and left only pleasant memories. "He was the one to teach me that song, did you know?"

Without a moment's hesitation, Lily began to hum a lingering, melodic tune.

"That's the same song you sang during karaoke, isn't it?"

Lily nodded as she rested her head against me again. "Mhm, I'm happy you remembered. It's a nice song, isn't it?"

"It is, but it's made all the nicer because you're the one singing it."

"You flatterer…" Lily said with a giggle, rolling her face against my shoulder.

"It's just the truth – you're sweet, thoughtful, caring…you're really amazing, Lily."

She slowly sat up as the two of us locked eyes, a new tension building between us.

"Yuu…"

Lily took my hand in hers, her fingertips tenderly approaching my wrist.

"Lily, I – "

I leaned forward, unthinking, as my hands reached past hers and ran along her waist.

"I, uh…I l–"

"Is everyone ready to depart?"

With a jolt me and Lily pulled away as Athena came down the stairs, Luna in her arms and Nina following shortly behind.

"Oh, um, yeah, sure. You ready to go, Lily?" I could feel my cheeks burning amidst my near-public confession.

"We...were not interrupting anything, were we?" Athena asked.

"No! No, really – "

"Mhm, we were just waiting for everyone," Lily said with exceptional calm. "Shall we?"

Athena eyed us carefully, but seemed satisfied enough with Lily's response and proceeded to load Luna onto my back (our now-usual arrangement for going out), as our merry group set out into the frigid winter air, headed for a night full of lights, warmth, and laughter.

24

"Ahh, so many good foods~" Nina let out a satisfied sigh as we exited the restaurant together. "Master should learn to cook like that too!"

"Now, now, don't be rude," Athena chided gently. "Yuu makes do with what facilities are made available to him, and we should all be appreciative for his efforts, whatever their results."

"I'm...not exactly sure that's a compliment."

"Th-that is, I only mean to promote an appreciation for the lengths you go to provide us with adequate comfort and necessity."

"It's alright, it's alright, I'm just teasing – plus I'm sure it wouldn't hurt for me to brush up on my cooking skills sometime."

I could hear Lily giggle beside me as Athena focused her gaze straight ahead, pressing onward with muted determination.

"Athena's right though, you really do a lot for us," Lily said as she grabbed my arm and pressed herself against me playfully. "I hope we can repay your kindness someday."

"Nah, not at all. If anything, I should be thanking you – I mean, I owe you my life after all."

"Yuu – "

"Not just literally!" I grimaced to myself as I reflected on what got me into this situation in the first place. "Up until I met all of you, I hadn't really been doing anything with my life. You've done a lot more than just give me my life back – you gave me a reason to live it." I leaned back as we continued walking and looked up at a twinkling night sky, shining dots splattered across an inky black canvas. "So if there's anything in it that I'm thankful for, it's you guys."

"Master really is sweet, even if he can be dumb sometimes... " Nina said softly.

I was about to protest her back-handed remark, but as the others gave their assent I decided it wasn't worth fighting. Plus, I knew deep down what she meant – I'd be the first to admit that I could be slow on the uptake when it came to other people's feelings, and this was made all the more difficult due to the fact that none of them were technically human. Sure, they looked human, and by this point had learned to more or less act human, but I think all of us remained keenly aware that there remained a fundamental difference in our existences.

"Oh, oh! Master, let's go in there!" Nina had regained her energetic cheerfulness as she pointed to a nearby store. It had a wide front, with large windows exposing an intricate display of Christmas toys and decorations, all blinking and moving along against the quiet hum of gears rotating and mechanical pieces meshing.

"I would not mind taking a brief reprieve in this area, should we have the time for it," Athena added somewhat bashfully.

"Sure, why not. That ok with you, Lily?"

Lily gave a quick nod as she took Nina's hand and led us into the department store. Immediately upon stepping through the automatic doors, we were greeted with a blast of warm air matched only by the onset of merry caroling, paraded from speakers all around the store. At any other time of year I might be inclined to say that this kind of overindulgence was stifling, even gaudy, but there was just something about Christmastime that made it so difficult to not get sucked into the festive atmosphere.

As the girls each took off in a different direction to explore, I decided I might as well try to get some shopping done myself while I was here. Christmas itself was only a few days away, and I was hoping I could get something nice for all of them; after all, so far as I understood, this was their first time really celebrating as residents of this world.

Wandering into the clothing department, I remembered that Nina only had a few outfits she rotated through on a regular basis. She hadn't given me any specific gift ideas earlier, and I doubted she would tell me what she wrote in her letter to Santa, so I was stuck going on instinct alone. As I scanned through rows of tops and dresses and jackets of every color and style and material imaginable, I felt with mounting dread someone tap my shoulder. It wouldn't be *completely* unusual for a guy to go shopping alone for women's clothes around this time (I mean, plenty of people had female friends and relatives they would buy clothes for, right?), but the last thing I wanted to do was needlessly draw attention to myself.

Slowly turning around, I was met with crashing waves of relief and apprehension as I saw Himeo standing there, hands behind her back and eyes brimming with devious curiosity.

"I know I've said before that you need to update your wardrobe," she said as joined me in looking through a nearby stack of shirts. "But this wasn't exactly what I had in mind. Still, to each their own~"

Yep. This was gonna go about as well as I expected.

"Good to see you too. Now was there something you needed, or did you just come over to pester me?" I asked as I tried to stay focused on the task at hand.

"Woah, woah, mister! No need for that kind of attitude. I just came over to see what you were doing out so late and say hi is all."

"Sorry, sorry, that was a bit harsh." I sighed and laid down the small white shirt I was holding, trying to place it back neatly but ultimately only crumpling it more in the process. "I'm just having trouble figuring out what kind of gifts to get everyone. I kinda know what they like, but I want each gift to come more from the heart, y'know?"

Himeo smiled and shook her head knowingly. "Did anyone ever tell you that you're as dumb as you are sweet?"

"Actually, that sounds kind of familiar –"

"Anyway, what I'm trying to say is: They'll love anything you get them, because it's a gift that came from you, that you picked out on your own. Just the fact that you thought of them probably means more than anything you could buy here."

"You really think so…?"

Himeo laid one hand on my shoulder and stared me in the eyes. "I'm a girl, and they're girls."

"Spirits," I tried to correct. "And a hybrid, I guess."

She shook her head. "No, that's just some label they're used to. Deep down, they're *girls*. And from one girl to one clueless boy, they're all crazy for you. So don't let them down for me, alright?"

I didn't doubt that they all cared for me, just like I cared about them, but I'd hardly go as far as to say they were *crazy* over me.

As Himeo turned to leave, I called out to her. "Hey, I know this might be asking a lot, but could you, uh, help me out a little more? You did a really good job picking out clothes for Athena and Lily, and so I was kinda hoping you could help me find something nice for Nina as well. I know it should come from me, but..." I threw up my hands, looking around. "I'm hopeless."

With a satisfied smile, Himeo strode over and patted me on the back. "You sure are, but what else are friends for?" She began carefully looking over a nearby pile of tops, whispering to herself as she went about the task. "Too small...too revealing... too plain...too cheap..."

Not wanting to be totally useless (though the longer this went on the more it seemed that was already the case), I began my own search, skimming through racks and rows of dresses. It was pretty easy to shop with the girls when they could pick out exactly what they wanted, but picking out a gift felt totally different – I wanted it to be something special, not just something they liked, and so somehow showing just how much they meant to me. Still dwelling on this conundrum, I didn't notice Himeo sneak around behind me.

"You sure seem to have a thing for dresses, don'tcha?"

Startled, I whipped around, holding on to one of the pieces placed in front of me.

"No, it's not like that, it's just..." I searched for the right way to express my feelings. "I shouldn't just give them something I think they'd like on their own, right? It should be something that has a little bit of me in it, too – something that connects us. And since Nina doesn't have any clothes like this, I thought it might be nice for her to have something to wear if we all go out together again sometime"

Himeo stared at me blankly, not responding.

"Sorry, I just realized how dumb that all sounded–"

She shook her head swiftly. "No, no, I was just surprised is all – I think that's the first time you've said something so thoughtful before."

"Alright, I don't think it'd be the *first* time–"

"Hey, that's actually a pretty nice one you picked out. And all on your own! It's like you didn't even need my help in the first place."

"Is it?" I held the dress up for a closer inspection, as I had just grabbed it aimlessly. It was somewhat simple, not unlike something Lily would wear, with a creamy orange blend. A cloth flower was affixed to the side of the front, which gave it a subtle, though nonetheless distinct, formality. "Yeah, y'know what? It is."

I smiled to myself, contented – even if I had picked this out at complete random, I still *had* picked it out. And if Nina really liked it and wore it, so much the better.

"Oh, sorry for stringing you along for a bit," I said with some embarrassment. "I think I have a better idea as to what to get for the others, so is there any way I can return the favor?"

Himeo waved her hands and laughed. "I'm good, I'm good, no need to worry." She paused, glancing off to the side. "Though there is one thing you can promise me."

"Sure, what is it?"

"Make sure you take good care of those girls, ok? I don't think I need to tell you this, but the closer people get to each other, the easier it is for one to hurt the other – even if they don't mean to."

"Wait, you think I'm gonna hurt them –?"

"No, no, it's nothing like that. I know you mean well, so it's just that..." For once, Himeo seemed genuinely apprehensive with her thoughts. "Sometimes your good intentions can actually end up hurting the people who care for you the most. So promise me you'll keep that in mind, alright?"

I still didn't understand what she was implying, but the middle of a department store didn't seem like the best place to be having a serious heart-to-heart, so I decided to just agree and let Himeo be on her way.

"Alright," I said to no one in particular as I gripped Nina's gift. "Where to next?"

Noticing the book department wasn't too far off, I headed in that direction and browsed through the labyrinth of titles, trying to find something that Athena might enjoy. After a bit of searching, I came across an entire history aisle, ripe with every topic one could think of. I was tempted to stay there and check a few out for myself, but time was short and the mission critical.

While flipping through some of the more interesting-looking volumes, including a collection of local folklore and a sort of encyclopedia of mythical creatures, I finally settled on two hefty tomes – one which went over techniques for maintaining backyard gardens, and another which looked at the development of classic weaponry. I thought they might be a little on the nose, but I was confident she would at least enjoy the subjects.

Next up was the entertainment department, which held an (admittedly small) anime section. I was a casual fan myself, with a few box sets at home, but Lily had already burned through them in no time and was always asking me to find more. I didn't recognize any of the titles being sold, so I had to rely on some vague descriptions on the backs of each cover, as well as the art style on the front. Fortunately, there was a sale going on at the time, so I was able to purchase a few that I thought she might like – two were typical high school romance series, while another, through some blend of action and comedy, follows a hero finding out he's not the one described in a prophecy to save the world. Given that Lily was the type of person (or spirit) to get so invested in the characters she was watching that any flaws a show might have would easily fade away, I was sure she'd like them regardless of any objective quality.

Finally, Luna – if I was being honest, she was by far the easiest to shop for. Since she had a... *penchant* for falling asleep in random places (whenever she did muster the energy to get up for a bit), getting her a small blanket and pillow she could carry around with her to soften any falls she did take seemed like an obvious choice. The linens section itself was somewhat out of the way, but it at least gave me a chance to see more of the store than I would have otherwise – I hadn't actually been to this department store many times, only once or twice when I was very young, so it was a good opportunity to see everything they had to offer.

Naturally, Christmas decorations and themed products dominated the store shelves, creating a palette of reds, greens, golds, and silvers that swirled together in an almost disorienting display of colors. Still, I had to admit it was all fairly nostalgic. Since there was no one else to decorate for at home, I usually kept things pretty sparse year over year; I had enough trouble keeping the place in one piece at times anyway, so decorating felt a bit superfluous. Now that I was living in a much fuller (and livelier) house, though, it made me kinda miss how things used to be when I was a kid. As I grabbed a fluffy pillow from a pile stacked haphazardly in a crate, as well as a blanket with a Christmas tree pattern, I made a mental note to ask the girls for help in prepping the house for the upcoming holiday.

25

"Thank you for shopping with us, and happy holidays!" The clerk gave a cheery wave as I gathered my purchases in a few nondescript paper bags and set out looking to gather the others.

I first stumbled into Lily, who was sitting in one of the book aisles, completely absorbed in a manga volume she had opened across her lap. I carefully snuck up beside her and poked her in the cheek, causing her to jolt back and almost knock me over.

I guess she was *really* into whatever she was reading.

"Ah, hey, sorry for startling you. I just wanted to see how you were doing, and let you know I'm ready to head home whenever everyone else is."

Lily's cheeks flared a bright pink, from what I thought at first was embarrassment at being surprised, but as she hurriedly closed the book and set it aside, I began to question my initial assumption.

"Uh, find anything good here?" I tried to ask casually.

"Yeah, there's some good stuff, nothing you'd like though I'm sure, anyway we can head out no need to stick around here."

It was plain to see she was being evasive, though that still left the obvious question – why?

"That's fine I suppose, but what were you reading? You seemed really into it. You didn't even hear me come u–"

I stopped mid-sentence as I noticed the cover of the book she had her hand over. A scantily-clad maid was in a..."compromising" position, with the words *Lustful Service* emblazoned in an elegant script.

"See! I told you it was nothing you'd be interested in." Lily laughed nervously as she hid the book behind her back. "Well I think we've seen all there is to see here time to go!" She stood up quickly and began to march forward mechanically, not daring to so much as glance behind her.

Watching her walk away, I had to shake my head and laugh. Lily had certainly come a long way from when we first met – for better or worse, she had been steadily adopting human social norms, which now appeared to include some level of bashfulness towards more intimate acts. Although a part of me felt bad that she was so self-conscious about these kinds of things now, I also had to admit that her shyness only made her cuter.

Soon after I caught back up to Lily, we were able to find the others in short order – Athena was inspecting some kitchenware and furniture that she thought we might be able to use (she proved herself to be pragmatic as ever, no matter the setting), while Nina had brought Luna over to the pet section to watch some of the small critters play around. Of all the girls, it seemed those two had grown the closest since we all started living together; I guess it helped that Nina was the only one of us who could really "talk" to Luna, even when she was sleeping. Still, I was happy she had that kind of companionship, and could even enjoy being in a world that effectively put such a burden on her.

"Hey you two, ready to leave?"

Nina nodded rapidly as Luna mimicked her much more

slowly and lazily, a perfect parallel between the two.

"But wait wait wait!" Nina blurted suddenly. "We're forgetting something super important!"

"Hm? What's that?"

"Our friend at home! You promised we would get him a gift, right master?"

Thinking back on our conversation earlier, I guess I had told her we'd find something. But what do you even get a monster for a gift? Do they even understand what a gift is? What could he use?

"I…guess you're right, but do you have any ideas as to what we should get?"

Nina nodded again, puffing out her chest proudly.

"Nina looked alllll around the store, and found the perfect gift right here – look!" She pointed to the plastic cage she was standing next to, which housed a few small, white mice.

"A…mouse?"

"Mhm! If our friend has a friend, then he won't have to be lonely anymore!"

I had to smile despite myself at Nina's warm innocence.

"Don't you think a mouse might be a little too small for something like that, though?" If the golem even understood what a pet was, I don't think there was any guarantee that it wouldn't just outright squish it by accident.

Nina shook her head, a pleading look in her eyes. "Nina knows he'll be gentle. He's a good monster, and he's very nice."

I still wasn't sure if Nina was able to communicate with the golem in the same way that she talked with Luna, but at this point I figured she knew better than I did on matters like this.

"Alright, I guess that's fine, if you think it'll like it."

"He will, Nina's sure of it!" She smiled triumphantly,

excitedly bouncing up and down as we purchased one of the mice and a basic pet care kit.

And so with all our errands taken care of, and everyone more or less tuckered out, we decided to finally head home. On our way, however, I noticed Athena keeping a respectable distance from the rest of us.

"Hey, everything ok?" I called out.

She seemed genuinely surprised by the question and nodded quickly.

"Yes, yes, everything is as it should be."

"You're walking awfully far from the rest of us, though. We didn't do anything to upset you, did we?"

"N-no, not in the slightest!" Athena's cheeks reddened slightly as she now shook her head frantically. "Truly, nothing is amiss – let it bother you no longer."

With a shrug, I decided to keep walking and let it be; if something really was on Athena's mind, and she felt like sharing it, I'm sure she'd do so when she felt ready.

"Oh! You didn't get to see our mousey friend, did you?" Nina said suddenly. She had been so excited after we bought the mouse that she insisted on carrying it all the way home for us. "That must be why Athena's so sad!"

Nina tried to move towards Athena, who stopped dead in her tracks and held her hand out, keeping Nina (literally) at arms-length.

"Do not take one step closer with that…beast!"

Puzzled by Athena's outburst, me and Lily stopped and looked to her.

"You don't mean –" Lily started.

"You're afraid –" I added.

"Of a mousey?!" Nina finished with what could only be

described as amazement crossed with befuddlement. "But you're so big, and he's so tiny and cute!"

"Would you perhaps be implying I am not cute?" Athena answered with grim intent. I wanted to point out the irony of her statement, but figured I had already suffered enough cuts and bruises as is.

Nina shook her head and giggled, holding the cage up to her face.

"It's just that he's such a friendly little mousey, Nina thought you might want to meet him too~"

"I can guarantee you with full assurance that I am living quite fulfilled without the presence of that creature anywhere near my vicinity."

"Aww, are you sure? Look, look~" Nina tried to hold the cage up closer to Athena, who bolted across the street in two massive strides.

"I...think you should just let her be," I said, patting Nina's head.

I thought Athena might eventually come back to join us for the rest of the walk home, but it seemed she had decided to wait until we actually reached the house to come near us again.

"I'm sorry we freaked you out so badly back there," I said with some amusement as I unlocked the door and let everyone inside. "I think Nina meant well, she just didn't know you were so afraid of mice. None of us did, now that I think about it."

Athena gave a defiant sigh and brushed past me.

"Hardly. A warrior such as I, afraid of a creature so small?" She turned around with dramatic grace, her skirt accentuating her movements. "I have slain dragons the size of mountains, met giants in nothing but bare-handed combat, and led entire armies to victory against odds that were nothing less than impossible." With each claim she had taken one step closer to us. "And yet you would propose that I harbor fear of a mouse – a mouse of all things! If you are to serve baseless accusations of my phobia, I would ask you at least do me the honor of making it dignified."

"Ah, sorry about that." Slowly I took the cage from Nina's hand. "Then you wouldn't mind holding him for a bit, right?"

I placed the cage between my and Athena's faces, causing her to run out of the room in a single instant.

"Yeah...I thought that might still be the case," I said with a laugh. "Anyway, what do you say we introduce our new friends to one other?"

Nina and Lily agreed enthusiastically, and so we entered the freezing night air once again to meet our resident golem, slumped against the fence in its usual position.

"Hey, uh..." After I had more or less given up trying to communicate with the monster, I hadn't thought much about how I addressed it. I looked to the two girls beside me (as Luna was now dozing on the couch). "We still haven't given it a name, have we?"

"Master..." Nina said shyly. "You keeping calling him an 'it,' Nina doesn't think that's very nice."

Come to think of it, Nina did exclusively refer to the golem as "he" whenever we talked about it.

"Ah, that's my mistake. Did it– I mean, did he tell you that he's a he?"

Nina nodded, beaming. "Mhm! That's why if we give the mousey a name, we should give him a name too!"

"It would certainly do better than trying to constantly refer to him in vague terms," Lily agreed.

"Alright, so what should we call him?"

Nina looked to Lily, Lily looked to me, and I looked to the mouse, which didn't seem keen on providing a suggestion any time soon.

"Well, how about..."

I wracked my brain trying to think of where we could come up with a name. It felt wrong to just give one at random, but I wasn't sure where to even start.

"Maybe...a book?" Lily offered.

Me and Nina turned to her, a bit confused as to what exactly she meant.

"Y'know, we could read through a book, and get some names from there. And he can tell us what he thinks, maybe?"

I looked to Nina with a shrug. "That works for me. Why don't we try again first thing in the morning?"

"Ok! Oh, but first – " Nina grabbed the plastic cage from my hands and, opening the latched top, carefully withdrew the mouse. "Here! For you!"

She held open her hands as the mouse scurried about, sniffing the fresh air and making sense of its new surroundings.

After a small delay the golem shifted in place, reaching out and opening its palm, to which the mouse readily scurried onto. The golem returned its hand on top of its knees and, using his other hand, created a makeshift shelter for the tiny creature.

"You think it'll be ok out here?" I asked hesitantly.

As if in response, the golem lifted its other hand to show the mouse curled up in a ball, sleeping peacefully.

"Nina thinks...he's saying he can keep his new friend warm!"

"I guess that leaves us to still take care of the feeding and cleaning," I said as I watched the golem return to its dormant state. "But if the two of them are happy like that, who am I to complain."

With a satisfied nod, Nina led the rest of us back inside, a careful excitement brewing as we wondered what name our friend might finally take in the morning.

* * *

"William? Henry? Francis?" Lily was flipping through a book on pirates, calling out a new name each time she found one. Nina kept looking to the golem, then shaking her head sadly.

"Sorry, he's not responding to any of them," she said softly.

"Is it possible he doesn't know what a name is?" I ventured. "It could be he's just confused as to why we're shouting out random words in front of him."

"No, no! Nina doesn't know for sure, but maybe…" She closed her eyes and seemed to be thinking hard about it. "She knows he appreciates the company at least!"

"That, uh, doesn't exactly answer my question," I murmured to myself. "Well anyway, why don't we head inside for a bit before we freeze? We can always come back in an hour or so and try again with some other books."

"I wouldn't mind that, to be honest," Lily said. "I feel bad leaving him out in the cold, but I think he can bear the weather a bit better than we can."

"Sounds good. I'll make some hot chocolate and grab some blankets to help us warm up – you coming, Nina?"

"Mm…" Nina appeared distracted by something as she looked towards the golem. "Can Nina get an extra blanket, too?"

"Of course, that's no problem. You must not be used to weather like this, huh?"

Nina shook her head.

"No no, it's not like that, master. He's cold too." She gestured to the golem, who hadn't stirred this entire time.

"Wait, really? I was thinking since he's made of...y'know, rock and all, he wouldn't feel things like cold."

"Nina isn't sure how it works, but she can tell he's a lot less active than he was before." Considering the golem barely moved when he first joined us, I can't imagine how she spotted that kind of difference. "If he warms up, maybe he'll help us find him a name!"

"I guess if we're just giving him some blankets, that should be fine." I glanced at the doorway, trying to size it up. Even if I really wanted to, there was still no way we could fit him inside. Blankets would have to do.

As I put some water on the stove to boil, Nina scurried around the house grabbing sheets and blankets and quilts of every size and material she could find. Lily had suggested we watch a show together, and even Athena came downstairs with Luna to join us while she read.

Leaning against the counter, I turned around to watch them all, so engrossed in their own little worlds, yet undeniably connected in this motley family of ours.

And at last, I smiled.

A smile of true, contented happiness.

These girls had come into my life by pure chance, had brought with them so much joy and so much pain, and I couldn't be more thankful for it all. They were each crazy, sweet, gentle, energetic, determined, insightful, silly, and naïve in their own way, and, though I couldn't quite describe it at the time, I understood they had already taught me more about myself than anyone else ever had.

With a satisfied sigh, I returned to the kettle and began

pouring water into mugs, four of a matching set lined up in a row. Was this what it meant to be happy? Was this what I was willing to fight for?

It had to be so.

Maybe it was selfish to live and die for such personal goals, but deep down I knew that wasn't the full of it. I wasn't happy just because of what these girls brought into my life – I was happy because I was able to see them go about *as* normal girls. To see them smile, and laugh, and cry, and feel however they would without fear of what tomorrow brings…that was worth protecting. That was worth it all.

"Yuu? Are you ready to start?" Lily was calling to me from the living room, having already popped in a DVD.

"Yeah, coming – just one sec."

I carefully loaded the mugs onto a tray and brought them out for everyone to enjoy. As I entered the living room I could see through the glass doors that our golem friend was covered in nearly every inch by blankets – Nina was nothing if not thorough in her efforts.

"Here you are," I said to Lily as I handed her a mug. "Just be careful, it's still hot."

"Thank you," she said sweetly, as I felt a brief wisp of cold and an unmistakable softness touch my cheek.

"You don't have to thank me, it was nothing…" I said awkwardly as I placed a mug in front of Athena.

Lily only giggled and threw her arms around mine, clinging tight to me as she sent shivers through my body in more ways than one; this newly discovered timidity returned once more, though I still couldn't understand why.

Sinking into the couch, I felt Nina drop her head against my lap, holding Luna close against her. As I was about to ask what she was doing, I could hear both girls' quiet breathing, suggesting she had fallen asleep as soon as she had nestled in. Lily was beaming at the two of them, smiling blissfully to herself as she stroked Nina's ears lovingly.

"Those two have really become inseparable, haven't they?" she said quietly.

I nodded slowly and continued to watch them – Nina had her arms and legs wrapped protectively around Luna, who had the faintest hint of a smile form on her lips as Nina shifted slightly and hugged her tighter. Seeing them together, I remembered Luna's cryptic questions one more time:

What is most important to you?

Who is most important to you?

Settling in place as Lily hit play on the remote, I rested my hand over hers. I think I'd finally found my answers.

26

"Merry Christmas!"

Rubbing the last of the sleep out of my eyes, I was greeted by the harmonious sound of the four girls' cheery (and in Luna's case, half-mumbled) holiday wishes.

"Hey guys, merry Christmas to you too."

The house had been persistently abuzz as the day itself approached, so there had been plenty of preparations to take care of. I'd snuck out to get some extra gifts for the girls and, last minute as it might've been, we were all able to get out and pick a tree (among the few stragglers left) to place in the living room. Nina's natural finesse was great for hanging lights up around the house and on the tree (though she had a penchant for getting distracted and ending up tangled inside them), while Lily and Athena had been practicing in the kitchen to learn some simple baking recipes. Now that the morning had finally arrived, it was easy to tell that their excitement had reached its peak.

"C'mon masterrr, it's already so late!" Nina pounced onto my lap, forcing me upright. I looked to the clock by the side of the bed – the digital display held a steady 6:00 AM.

"Uh, you do know this is even earlier than when we usually get up?"

"But today is Christmaaas!" Nina scrambled off my lap and started hopping from one foot to the other as she circled around the room, singing "It's Christmas it's Christmas it's Christmas~" all the while.

Looking to Lily, I couldn't help but smirk. "At least there's no second-guessing what day it is, huh?"

She giggled slightly and wrapped her fingers around mine as she gently tugged me towards the edge of the bed. "She's right though, there's lots we want to do today, so the earlier we start the better."

"In all things expediency is best, when possible," Athena added as she patted down my bedhead.

To be fair, I had promised them quite the full day – we'd start by opening presents in the morning, then I'd make a full breakfast feast, after which we'd gather on the couch to watch some movies, and order in some food in the evening. I had asked if they were sure they didn't want me to make something special for dinner, but they insisted that they'd rather just spend the evening relaxing together. As much as I came to enjoy having them around, it was nothing if not draining (be it an attack from some otherworldly creature or just getting through day-to-day activities), so I was all but too happy to take a little break like that myself.

"Ok, ok, let's get going and see what Santa left for everyone," I said with a yawn.

"Santa? He came?!" Nina stopped in her tracks, dumbfounded.

"You have been good this year, right? I see no reason why he wouldn't have stopped by."

Without another word, Nina grabbed my wrist and began dragging me towards the door. Despite her small size she could be surprisingly strong, especially when something as important as gifts were on the line.

"Woah, woah, they're not going anywhere. Just give me a second to throw on a sweatshirt, and I'll come right down with everyone."

Nina paced in front of the door as I threw on a simple grey hoodie and scooped Luna out of bed – it seemed that all the excitement so early in the morning had drained what little energy she had stored up, and she promptly fell back asleep as I was climbing out of bed. Lily, for her part, had helped keep Nina entertained in the days leading up with even more fantastical stories about Santa Claus, which was partly to blame for her present eagerness.

"Alright, let's begin the first official Risher family human-spirit Christmas celebration!" I announced as we exited the bedroom.

"...Title's still a work in progress," I added sheepishly amidst the girls' bemused and incredulous stares.

Finally descending the stairs, we were met with a dazzling display of lights and tinsel, soft multicolor hues mixed with shimmering silver and gold. Under the tree were an assortment of gifts, each wrapped neatly and precisely (courtesy of Athena) and topped with a unique bow (thanks to Lily and Nina, the latter of whom seemed more interested in playing with the ribbons than actually tying them).

"Wooooow~" Nina's voice was filled with innocent awe, her eyes shimmering as she took in the whole display in its full effect for the first time.

"To those who work diligently, may they reap the greatest rewards," Athena said with a satisfied smile.

"Yeah...it really does look amazing." Thinking back to how

I'd spent most of my Christmases in the past, this was like stepping into another world – or another time. "Even if it's a little premature, I need to say thank you – really, thank you everyone."

From the haphazard placement of ornaments on the tree, to the scattered blankets and pillows from preparations late into the night, to the carefully lined stockings against the wall –

"Hm? What for?" Lily asked.

"This place finally feels like a home. Not because of how we dressed it up – I mean, that's nice for sure. But right here, right now, I can see we really are a family. So even though it's still early, I guess I can say my Christmas wish already came true."

I felt a hand reach over my head and pull me into a now-familiar softness.

"You are perhaps too tender and kind-hearted for the challenges we face, yet it remains my dearest hope you never abandon such honest sentiments," Athena spoke gently as she ran her fingers through my hair.

"Um, thanks, but it's really no big de–"

"It's true!" Lily added as she wrapped her arms around my middle and rested her head against my shoulder. "I couldn't ask for a better boyfriend or family to share~"

"I don't think you share boyfri–"

"Nina loves master too!!" Nina exclaimed as she jumped into our group hug, sending us toppling to the floor in a heap.

Groaning from the sudden impact, I was about to pick myself up until I saw Luna woozily standing over us.

"Yuu…nice…" she managed to whisper, before falling down onto the rest of us.

With a strained laugh, I tried to push myself up, but found myself thoroughly pinned to the floor.

"As nice as this, I think we should start to get up now."

Lily nuzzled her face against my chest. "Mm mm, I'm fine here."

The fact that none of the other girls budged an inch seemed to confirm they felt the same way.

Now, I wasn't one to be unappreciative when held down by four beautiful women, but this wasn't exactly the most comfortable or ideal of situations. Plus, after spending every night cramped in the same bed with everyone, the initial novelty had quickly worn off.

"Sure, sure, but if I don't get up I can't give you all your presents, right?"

Nina bounded to her feet, ears perked.

"Nina forgot! We have to open presents let's go let's go go!"

With that declaration, she dropped back onto her knees and placed her hands on her lap, still as could be.

"I guess we shouldn't keep her waiting…" Lily teased as she pushed herself off me, guiding Luna onto her lap as I helped Athena to her feet.

I shuffled over to the tree, where an assortment of boxes and bags covered in striped foil and festive designs were spread out before us. I had to admit to feeling a bit of pride in the array, if for no other reason than I could finally express my gratitude in some small way.

"Ok, let's see who's first…" I scanned across the labels, seeing if any jumped out at me. "Since she's been so patient, why don't we start with Nina."

Nina nodded her head in silent and rapid agreement.

Reaching through an opening in the gift pile, I picked out a flat, rectangular box, with a smaller square lying on top and handed it to her.

"Merry Christmas, Nina."

Nina swiftly tore through the packaging with unsuppressed enthusiasm, as if enjoying the mere act of tearing off the wrapping paper as much as opening the gift itself. When she finally got through both boxes, her eyes widened as she let out a long "Ohh!"

"Do you like them?" I asked with some apprehension.

"It's beautiful, master!!" In one motion, Nina hugged the dress to her chest and launched herself at me, nearly knocking me to the ground again. She suddenly pulled back, however, as she carefully examined the simple red ribbon laid over the dress.

"And this…?" she asked quietly.

"Oh, yeah – I was thinking you could put your bell on that, maybe wear it like a necklace or bracelet."

"Do you really mean it?" Her voice was now just above a whisper.

"Of course. It might not be much, but I hope it shows my feelings for you and appreciation for all you've done."

Nina blushed fiercely as she hid her face behind the dress and muffled out, "Can she wear it now, please please? Can she?"

"Sure, sure, just make sure to get changed in the bedroom first," I said as I tussled her hair. Nina had a habit of…*missing* a few crucial steps when she got excited about something.

"Mhm, Nina will be right back!" I watched as she skipped away, chanting to herself "A dress from master, a dress from master, a dress for Ni-na~" all the way upstairs.

Lily and I couldn't help but let out another laugh at her innocent exuberance; even Athena let slip a small smile herself as she listened to the merry chant.

"Oh! And this is for you." I felt around under the tree and pulled out two sizeable packages and brought them over to where Athena was sitting. "I hope you like it."

"Really, now!" Athena seemed almost offended by the gesture, but took the gifts anyway, if somewhat gingerly. "If any one should be offering their generosity, it is I to you for the staunch effort you have put forth thus far, in facing such monumental tasks heaped upon you–"

I waved her off before things got even more out of hand. "It's Christmas, of course I was gonna get you a gift. Now go on, open it."

"Very well, I suppose it would go against your nature should you have censored yourself from such a practice, but still –" Athena stopped mid-sentence when she saw what was hidden behind the wrapping paper. "Oh..." she said quietly as she caressed the cover of the gardening book, tracing her finger along each letter of the title. "Perhaps I was not alone in observing the habits of those close to me," I could barely hear her say as she continued to explore the tome.

Lily took my hand and squeezed gently, a seeming affirmation that this gift was a success, too.

Before I could do anything else, Athena spoke up again, not turning her face away from the book. "Lily, if I could –?"

Without a word, Lily nodded cheerily, as Athena stood up and walked over to us. I felt my heart quicken as she bent down towards me, her long, blonde hair practically creating a curtain around the two of us. I wanted to say something, but I knew all that would come out were half-stammered utterances, so I decided to keep my mouth shut and trust the two of them.

"I graciously thank you for your generosity and thoughtfulness – not only towards those you seek to protect, but the individual consideration you have bestowed upon each of us. It is a small token of my affection, though I hope its meaning bears true."

With her perplexing confession, Athena brushed her lips against my cheek, their slight warmth and ethereal softness causing me to freeze up. For all the times she had been so close and displayed some level of affection (intentional or not), this once again felt...different.

As this unmoving moment finally came to an end, Athena abruptly stood up and turned her back to us.

"I-I think I shall go give to these a proper place, and not add to the clutter of the room." With that, she grabbed both books from the side table and strode upstairs and away.

"That was, uh...nice," I mumbled, as Lily responded only with an equal parts mysterious and mischievous grin. "Anyway, let's see..." I moved around some of the gifts, of which a reasonable pile still remained. "How about...this one."

I had to admit that I had more or less given up trying to wrap Luna's gift – as I found through repeated trial and error, there really wasn't a great way to wrap a blanket and pillow and not make it look like an amorphous mess (unless you had a box the proper size, which I was quick to find I did not). Figuring she had her eyes closed 99% of the time anyway and wouldn't really mind, I just wrapped a ribbon around the edges and placed a bow on top, which at least gave it a reasonably festive feel.

I wanted to give it to Luna personally, but she was still fast asleep on Lily's lap, her small chest barely rising with each breath.

"I guess we'll just make use of them now, huh?"

"I think she'd appreciate it," Lily said with a giggle, carefully cradling Luna's head underneath her interlaced fingers and lifting up just enough so I could slip the pillow underneath and tuck the blanket around her.

Neither Lily nor I said anything for some time – I think we were both transfixed by the sort of tranquility Luna brought with her. No matter the situation, no matter the danger, she always seemed so peaceful. Even if she was still largely an enigma in many ways, none of us could deny her place in this home in the slightest.

"It's really something..." Lily said as she brushed a strand of Luna's hair off her cheek.

"What is?"

"Out of all the places in the universe, all the different people and spirits and creatures that exist, we all somehow ended up here. It has to be more than coincidence, right?"

Lily looked to me earnestly, as no clear answer presented itself in my mind. It did seem pretty strange that we would all grow so close in such a short time, but was that really due to anything more than circumstance and luck?

"I think...it's a little of both."

"Both?"

"Yeah, like..." I searched for the right way to say this. It was hard trying to describe things you never felt before, and ideas you'd never pondered. "Maybe it was chance that me and you first met. Maybe it was even the same for all of us meeting each other. But I don't think we're still here because of that – there's definitely something more there."

"Like fate?" Lily's question again gave no indication as to what whether she thought this was true or not – she was genuinely asking for my thoughts, so I was free to be as honest as I could.

"Maybe not quite as strong, but I don't think it'd be wrong

to call it that. I guess I'd say it's sort of like a…faith. You placed your faith in me, I placed my faith in you. We trusted each other – as did all our other friends who've joined us now. It's something no amount of random chance or good fortune could make up. It only happened because we really cared about each other, and because we wanted to see this through."

"Faith…" Lily seemed to be testing the word, as if this was her first time really hearing it. "Did you know that people's faith is strongest when they face the unknown?"

"You mean before they…die?"

She shook her head, a bittersweet smile on her lips. "Not necessarily, though I'm sure you know that's what I'm most familiar with." Lily turned her head to look me directly in the eyes, her gaze unwavering. "Still, when people have the answers they're seeking, when they've found what they're looking for, do they still have that faith? Or does it go away?"

Despite the meaning of her words, I felt no sadness or despair from Lily. As had become typical when we talked about bigger or emotional things, she spoke plainly and with full earnestness. Maybe she never thought to put up barriers around these oft-sensitive topics, or maybe she just never wanted to.

"I'm not sure, honestly." Lily pursed her lips and seemed like she was about to speak again, so I quickly placed one finger over her lips to pause her. "But however you look at it, what we have here is real. When we've finished what we set out to do – find love, find answers, find a home – this won't go away. That's not just faith, that's a fact."

As a few tears slipped down her cheek, Lily nodded and brought her face close to mine. Meeting her halfway, I rested my head against hers and held her face in my hands, wiping away the reticent stream that spoke so much more profoundly than anything either of us could say out loud.

After what must have only been a minute or two, yet felt like touching upon a quiet eternity in our own separate company together, I rustled Lily's shoulder and nodded towards the tree.

"There's still one person who hasn't gotten a gift yet."

She smiled as she rubbed her eye with her sleeve. "You know you didn't have to get me anything – just getting to be with you like this is the best gift I could have ever hoped for."

I handed her a small box wrapped in metallic violet paper and chuckled. "You're my girlfriend, of course I'd get you a gift."

"Girlfriend..." We had technically been "dating" since we first met, but it seemed like Lily had only just now realized it. "Girlfriend," she repeated with a satisfied smile.

Without further hesitation, Lily carefully peeled back the corners of the wrapping paper, making sure not to tear any part of it. As she gently pulled the paper away, she lifted up the first box to examine it closely, a new brightness shining in her eye.

"Where did you find this?" she asked abruptly, looking to me with a startling intensity.

"Uh, just at the department store, a few days ago. I kinda picked it out without knowing much about it, so I hope–"

"I've been looking everywhere for this! They only printed a few copies because the series wasn't popular, so it's kind of a collector's dream to find this." She seemed to catch herself and looked back at me with some embarrassment. "Or, um, so I've heard."

"So I take it you like it?"

"No matter what you got me, I'd cherish it forever," Lily said, clutching the box to her chest. "But yes, even beyond that this gift is amazing!" She threw her arms around my neck in an unusually warm embrace, careful not to smother Luna as she leaned forward.

I had to say I was pretty relieved that this all went over so well, though I was still confused as to how I'd found such a rare DVD set in a department store of all places. Maybe it was misplaced, or got mixed in with the more normal supply and got stocked? I mean, I didn't know anything about it myself, so I guess it stood to reason that unless another uber-fan like Lily went looking there for it, no one would think twice about some random show sitting on a shelf.

"There's...one more thing I'd like to give you." Lily looked at me curiously, tilting her head. "It's been a long time coming, but I think I'm finally ready." Again I felt my heart begin to race, as if standing at the edge of a precipice. I knew how I felt for Lily – or at least, knew I felt *enough* for her – and it was time to express that. "You're very special to me. More than a friend, more than family, something I can't really put words into. Except to say that I l–"

knock knock

From the kitchen I could hear a soft rapping at the door, as if someone was timidly checking to see if anyone was home.

"Oh? Are we expecting guests today? Your parents?" Lily asked.

"N-no, they said they couldn't get any time off of work. A-and anyway! It might've just been the wind, so, uh..." This wasn't exactly going as planned, but I was sure I could still salvage the mood. "What I was trying to say is–"

BAM BAM BAM

The knocking (or perhaps more appropriately, pounding) returned much more forcefully.

"I don't think that's just the wind," Lily said, placing a hand on my arm.

With a resigned sigh, I stood up and headed towards the kitchen. I guess this would have to wait until later.

"It's probably just someone asking for directions, I'll be right back."

Undoing the latch to the door, I could overhear muffled whispers – though I couldn't make out what exactly they were saying, it was easy to make out the difference: one voice was soft and measured, the other much harsher and insistent.

"Hi, how can I help –"

As I opened the door, my words caught in my throat. Standing in front of me were two girls. The one in front had fiery red hair done in twin tails, though my eyes were more immediately drawn to the pair of unmistakable wings behind her. The other – with her furry ears, swaying tail, vibrant brown hair, and round, curious eyes – was the spitting image of Nina herself.

27

"Alright, we gave him a chance to explain himself, so now we do things my way," the red-haired girl declared abruptly.

"I'm sorry, who are you ag–"

I was cut off by a knee coming straight for my abdomen. Thankfully Athena's training had paid off, and because the girl's sudden attack was still fairly telegraphed, it was easy enough to step to the side so that she missed wildly, causing her to lose her balance and fall flat onto the floor.

"I told you there was no need for violence..." the brown-haired girl said gently as she knelt down by her companion.

"Yeah, well, you were the one who insisted we come here in this form. It's so awkward to move around like this. If we went with *my* plan –"

"You would have burnt this kind gentleman's house down, gotten us killed, and possibly harmed my daughter, yes. And that is why we avoided it." The brown-haired girl kept a complete sense of calm in her voice, but even I could sense the threatening iciness hiding just beneath. For all that she looked like Nina, the differences in personality were already starkly apparent.

The brown-haired girl seemed to finally take notice of the situation she and her friend had (quite literally) fallen into and looked up at me. "I apologize for my companion's impolite introduction. You see, I'm looking for my daughter, and – being unfamiliar with this area – have searched around for some time. It was only by chance we ran into a friendly stranger who pointed us to your home."

"Your...daughter?" All at once, it clicked – as unbelievable as it may be, this had to be Nina's –

"Momma?"

As Nina's voice suddenly came forth, I turned around to see her, Lily, and Athena standing in the kitchen doorway, disbelief and confusion spread across their faces.

"I heard some manner of tumult, so I thought to check on the circumstances, but it seems –"

Before Athena could finish, Nina had bolted past, throwing herself into the brown-haired girl's arms.

"Momma, it is you! It is!" For some time everyone remained silent, allowing Nina's muffled sobs and (what was now confirmed to be) her mother's gentle reassurances to be the only noise that filled the room.

"I'm guessing you probably have a lot of questions for us," I ventured after enough time had passed and emotions began to settle down.

Still caressing Nina's hair, her mother gave a peaceful smile. "I suppose you would for us as well. Although it may be a bit redundant at this point, would you mind if we come in?"

"Oh, yeah – please do. Let me get the door, you both are probably freezing." I hastily shut out the cold air and led our two guests to the living room. "Can I get either of you something to drink?"

"Tea would be lovely, if you have it," Nina's mother said, not taking her eyes off her child for even a moment.

"And for your friend…?"

The red-haired girl simply turned away in a huff, crossing her arms as she sat next to Nina's mother.

"Well, I'll set out an extra cup in case you're interested. Wouldn't do you any good to catch a cold, after all."

"Mm, I'll grab some extra blankets," Lily suggested, as Athena followed me into the kitchen.

"Have you already decided to place your trust in these strangers?" she asked in a hushed voice once we were a safe distance away.

"Nina said she was looking for her mom for some time, and the resemblance alone is pretty uncanny. Plus, it seemed like she recognized her in an instant, so I doubt it's a case of mistaken identity."

"Be that as it may, does this not all strike you as too convenient?"

"Maybe, but do you really think they came here to hurt us?" I asked plainly. To any other person it might have sounded harsh, even sarcastic, but when it came to addressing the unknown, I had grown accustomed to Athena's wariness.

Athena bit her lip and eyed the four girls in the living room (Luna having made a comfortable bed of the floor to the side). "No, I must admit not. If they were to arrive under false pretenses, I believe their actions and manner of speaking would have laid that bare."

Leaning against the counter, I watched Nina, her mom, and her apparent friend casually talking together. Nina seemed to be speaking at a mile a minute, while her mom only smiled blissfully as her friend tried to keep up.

"You're still thinking about what happened a few weeks ago, aren't you?"

Athena nodded solemnly. "From the smallest skirmish, to the largest war, knowledge of one's enemy is critical to not only success, but security as well. Given how little we yet know of Whitehearst, our understanding of those nefarious forces still unseen remains an even greater weakness." With a sigh, she closed her eyes and dropped her head. "I hope you may look past my critical assessment, and not mistake it for ill-intended distrust."

"Nah, I know you're not like that. I'm glad I have someone like you looking out for me, since an extra dash of caution is probably healthy, all things considered."

Athena gave a shy smile as she walked back to the living room. "You must be careful how you so freely say such things – a heart may yet be swayed where it holds no quarter. Still, I thank you for your understanding."

Given all that had transpired between us (including and especially this morning), even someone as dense as me could understand what she was really trying to say. Whether – and even how – I could reciprocate those feelings would have to wait, however. An even more pressing issue had arrived at our doorstep and was now waiting in the other room.

After filling up the mugs with water, I gathered them on a nearby wooden tray and stepped back into the living room, where Lily and Nina were catching her mother up on how they all ended up here in the first place.

"It certainly seems our host is no stranger to surprises," Nina's mother said as I came in.

"Yeah, I guess that's one way to put it," I said with a nervous laugh. Between random attacks from monsters and mages and trying to keep the girls' true nature a secret, I kinda wished "surprises" were the only thing I had to worry about.

"Oh, but that reminds me – I don't think I ever got your names," I said as I set down two festive-themed red and green mugs in front of our guests

Nina's mother giggled to herself and glanced at her friend, who only stared forward contemptuously. "I suppose in our excitement I did neglect the most basic formalities. My name is Maria, and my companion here – well, she can introduce herself, I'm sure."

The other girl's eyes narrowed as she watched over me, unblinking. "I have no reason to lower myself to pleasantries with some *human*." She practically spat out the last word, a singe of venom dripping off the last syllable.

Confused, I looked back at Maria, who shook her head, her smile never fading in the slightest. "You'll have to forgive her coarse introduction – despite my best efforts, Ruby still associates all mortals with the genealogy of mages, and therefore is...less than friendly towards them."

"They share the same bloodline, and thus carry the same sins. I see no reason to place my trust in those who'd sooner see me locked up or killed than even spoken to," Ruby muttered to herself.

Given Nina's personal history, it was fairly easy to figure out what she was referring to. I'm sure there was still plenty more to the issue that I didn't know or understand, but this didn't seem to be the ideal time to go asking about it.

"I can't speak too much to my defense, considering I still don't know a whole lot about where you come from or what it's like there, but I hope you can still take some comfort here, for what it's worth." Ruby remained silent, which, after what'd already been said, felt like the closest thing to a positive response I could hope for.

"Ruby, you have to be nicer to master!" Nina protested suddenly. "He took good care of Nina, and, um, I want you both…" Her cheeks reddened as she began to stumble over her words.

Ruby's eyes softened and a genuinely sweet smile crossed her lips. "Right, right – I won't make a big fuss for you and your betrothed. I don't know what you see in a mortal like that, but I'll support you regardless."

It was nice to see Ruby may have a kinder side after all, but it was a little strange to see her do such a sudden –

"I'm sorry – did you say betrothed?"

"Master! Don't say it out loud like that, you'll make Nina shy…" She covered her face with her hands and shook her head back and forth, stifled giggles creeping through all the while.

I looked around the room for some kind of explanation, but none seemed to be forthcoming.

"I'll admit I was a bit surprised when Nina explained she was already living with her mate," Maria said plainly. "Yet seeing how kind you've been to not just her, but the other individuals who have taken residence here as well, my mind has been at peace." Nodding to herself, she picked up the mug and took a long sip, as the rest of us only managed a stunned silence.

"Wait you didn't –" I started.

"Actually suggest –" Athena added.

"They're m-married?!" Lily finished with uncharacteristic fervor.

Maria looked up from her drink and scanned the room, blinking in surprise. "Of course – I thought he proposed just today, didn't he?"

The combination of Athena's icy stare with Lily's anxious confusion was overwhelming. If I didn't find a way to defuse the situation, things could get, uh...bad.

"Nina, you know what really happened, right?"

She probably just got mixed up in talking to her mom, or Maria herself misunderstood what she was really trying to say. Come to think of it, I still really wasn't sure how I'd categorize my relationship with most of these girls – I said we were family, and me and Lily were dating, but was there still something more to it all? Something different? Though I supposed now was hardly the right time to try and figure that out.

Looking down and tapping her fingers together, Nina spoke quietly. "Nina's still not sure why you picked her, but master said those were his feelings when he gave her this." She lightly flicked the bell that now hung from a wide ribbon around her neck, held by a neat bow tied in the back.

"I...still don't really follow."

"How can you lay claim to him as your own so suddenly, and without proper remediation?" Athena blurted, before catching herself and steadying her tone. "What I mean to say is, I do not believe any of us are aware of the relationship between that item and your supposed engagement."

Maria held up a hand. "I believe I can explain. You see, in the klarid culture, when one wishes to propose to their mate, they present two gifts – a token to mark their time together, and a cloth to bind them. By giving her such a gift, well..."

All eyes turned to Nina, who was absent-mindedly playing with the bell, as if lost in a trance. When she realized the pressure of the entire room was placed squarely on her, she snapped back to attention, looking around frantically.

"Huh? What? Did Nina do something wrong?"

"No, no, nothing like that," Lily said with a relieved sigh. "It's just...I think you might've been mistaken. Yuu wasn't trying to propose to you – er, right?" She looked at me with some sense of trepidation, which was quickly dispelled as I offered a swift nod in return.

"That's right," I said as I crouched down and placed a hand on Nina's head. "I'm sorry if I gave you the wrong idea. I really do care about you, I just...don't think I'm ready to get married yet. To anyone, honestly."

Nina returned to playing with the bell, her voice hushed. "So master...doesn't want to be with Nina?"

"No, no, that's not it at all. I would never want to be apart from you – from anyone here. You help make our house complete, you make me feel whole, too. I'm sorry if that's not exactly the answer you were hoping for, but I hope you can still accept my feelings."

With a shy smile Nina closed her eyes and nodded. "Nina wasn't sure if she was ready to be with master like that either." Looking under her bangs, she spoke so quietly that, even being right next to her, I could barely hear. "But one day, ok?"

Smiling despite myself, I nodded back. "One day."

"It seems that's settled at last," Maria said, bringing me back to the fact that I was still sitting in a room surrounded by other people.

"Sort of," I said hesitantly. "You mentioned something about Claire-ed earlier? What's that?"

Ruby, who up to this point had been more or less silent, let out an indignant snort. "You bring someone into your house and don't even know about where they come from? Next you'll tell me you call us all hybrids or something."

"Not. At. All." My reply was as automatic as it was mechanical, and though Athena was out of sight, I could feel her restraint in holding her tongue. I made a mental note to ask her more about this "discrepancy" later.

"Now, now – there's no need to squabble, it's entirely understandable." Maria spoke sweetly and at her own pace, as if a single trouble couldn't be impressed upon her. "As I'm sure you're already aware, Nina was raised as a captive all her life. All she knows about the outside world, and the culture of her people, came from stories I told her."

"Momma, you mean…?"

Maria nodded. "Those bedtime stories I told you when you were just a youngling were true – the race we come from, the klarid, span across many places, in many worlds. Over the years our numbers have diminished, but…" A dark cloud seemed to pass over Maria's pleasant countenance, though it vanished as quickly as it came. "Enough of these dark ruminations on the past." Squeezing Nina tight in her arms, she kissed the top of her head. "It has been many years since I last saw you, and I won't make the same mistake again. I love you, my precious daughter."

Nina rested her head against her mom's chest, closing her eyes. "Nina loves you too, momma."

Watching the two of them like that reminded me that each of these girls had had their own separate lives before stumbling into this world. Although it felt like we were building our own kind of future here, that didn't and couldn't take away from the places and pasts they came from.

Nina lifted her head again and looked up at Maria curiously. "Why *did* you leave Nina though? She was so lonely while you were away…" She cast her attention to the girl sitting next to her. "Ruby too! You stopped visiting, and never told Nina why."

"It's not like I wanted to! I told Maria – er, your mom, that we could take you with us. She said it'd be too dangerous, and that we'd come back to get you one day."

Nina looked back at Maria, who nodded solemnly.

"It was the most painful decision I've ever had to make. However, I knew that if we were caught trying to escape, we'd all suffer the consequences together. It was much safer to find a way out myself first, and return for you when we had a secure place to take you to."

"That's so sad..." Lily whispered, as Athena hugged her to her side.

"So...what happened?" I asked cautiously.

"As I've no doubt you are aware, the lands of men tend to be inhospitable toward those foreign to themselves." Although her voice didn't waver in the slightest, the strain of long-concealed pain lingered just behind her cheerful countenance. "We – that is, Ruby and I – tried our best to conceal the more...obvious elements of our heritage. With no resources and no place to call home, we wandered further and further from the place that was as much a home as prison."

"But how did you even end up in our world to begin with?"

"Hmph, like some dumb otherworlder would understand," Ruby declared indignantly.

"What she means to say," Maria corrected gently, "is that we are not certain ourselves."

Ruby's cheeks reddened as she glared at me – I wanted point out that I wasn't the one who called her out on this, but I was pretty sure that would just make the whole situation worse.

Nina touched Ruby's shoulder and looked at her entreatingly. "Where did you go, Ruby? Nina wants to know too."

With just those words, Ruby's expression changed completely once more. With a wide smile and a somewhat-embarrassed laugh, she rubbed Nina's head and began to explain. "Me and your mom looked around a lot, trying to find somewhere that'd be safe to bring you. I could kinda remember a place like that from when I was real little, so I thought maybe there'd be some more of us still hiding out in that area."

"And...did you find anyone?" Lily asked.

Ruby shook her head plainly. Despite her earlier aggressiveness, she showed no sign of anger or frustration now – it was as if this implied tragedy was nothing more than a fact of life, no more strange or upsetting than saying the sky was blue or the Earth was round. And so with that, I could sense her unspoken follow up: "It just is what it is."

"We did stumble upon an odd structure, however," Maria added after a brief pause.

"Oh?" Athena asked, leaning forward.

"It was just some big dumb rock," Ruby said dismissively. "There's a bunch of them all over where I come from. It's nothing special."

Athena seemed to be eyeing Ruby carefully, while Lily turned to me. "Yuu – doesn't that sound familiar?"

"Familiar?" I tried to think back on any big rocks we might have encountered, but nothing was jumping out at me. "I mean our friend outside is a big rock, but that's probably not what you mean."

Lily shook her head emphatically. "Mm mm, it was during the Lunar Festival. At least, I think..."

As Lily rested her chin on her hands, searching across her memories, Athena spoke up again.

"Could I trouble you to expound upon your discovery a bit further?"

Ruby let out a sigh and shrugged. "I've already told you pretty much everything we saw. We were looking around what used to be my home, and found some big stone pillar. It had some weird markings on it, but since neither of us could read it, we just left it alone."

"Are you certain that is all?"

Ruby glared at Athena. "Are you trying to say I'm a liar?"

Without breaking her gaze, Athena shook her head. "Not in the slightest. I trust your account fully – I only asked for clarification as there may be some significance to what you discovered."

Having expected a fight, Ruby seemed a bit taken aback by Athena's even-keeled response. "Yeah, well, I guess there was one other thing…" she murmured.

28

All eyes turned to Ruby expectantly.

As soon as she noticed the sudden change in attention, she began to squirm in place, tears welling up in the corners of her eyes. "Well you don't all have to stare at me like that!"

"It's ok dear," Maria said soothingly as she wrapped one arm around Ruby. "They're just invested in what you have to say – we all are."

"All this over some stupid human…" Ruby muttered to herself as she regained her composure.

At this point I had resigned myself to the fact that I would carry the blame – real or imagined – for all her problems while she was here.

"The only weird thing I can think of," Ruby began, closing one eye as she thought back on the day. "Is that both of us started feeling kinda tired after we found that monument or whatever it was. We decided to call it a day, and set up camp in a clearing in the nearby woods. When we woke up the next morning though, we were, well – here."

Ruby shrugged, still uncertain as to where "here" even was.

"I don't even know if the two things are related. When I was little, I remember the elders talking about some untapped magic or whatever in the area, but it didn't make any sense.

There was never anyone from our tribe who could use magic, so why would we even have something like that?"

Despite her typical assertiveness, Ruby seemed to be asking a genuine question; a rare sign of openness – and maybe even trust – towards us? I quickly corrected myself by noting that any perceived affinity she had was surely placed in the other girls, and so excluded me. I did remember how Nina felt a connection with all the spirits here – especially Luna – so maybe just like humans were close to mages, even different tribes were close to spirits? This line of thought was interrupted by a sudden exclamation from Lily.

"Luna!"

Everyone turned to her, puzzled.

"Uh, what about her?" I asked.

"That's where we saw a rock thing, right? Just like Ruby described – it was a sort of pillar, with markings all over it. We found Luna sleeping there the night of the festival."

Despite the vague description, I felt she was on to something. I mean, it was possible we were mixing up two totally different things here (it's not like Ruby and Maria's descriptions were any more specific), but it seemed like a line of investigation worth pursuing.

"Yeah, I guess you're right…" I started carefully, not sure where this was headed. "But how do you think that relates to what those two found?"

"I…hadn't thought that far ahead," Lily said somewhat sheepishly, rubbing the back of her head. "But I have a really strong feeling about this. There has to be something there – there must be. Call it spirit's intuition!" She puffed out her chest, proud of this not-quite-conclusion.

"It is possible…" Athena said distractedly, as if still lost in her own thoughts. "Mind you well, it remains only a possibility, yet I believe this discovery may be the thread that guides and binds us all."

A sense of anxious anticipation was building within the room.

"What do you mean?" Maria asked at last, as the unbroken silence weighed heavily upon us.

Athena snapped back to attention and looked around the room, like she just came out of a daze.

"Oh, um, my apologies. Where to begin…" After a brief pause, she nodded to herself and continued. "There is one common element unique to all of us here, no?"

"Oh Nina knows!" Nina blurted out cheerfully. "It's Yuu~" She swung her arms around my neck and nestled up against my shoulder, half on her mother's lap, half on me. I could feel Ruby's stare piercing through me, but tried to ignore it for the time being.

Athena giggled and nodded. "Yes, I suppose that's true, though there is something more to it – how we all arrived." She scanned each of the other spirits' faces carefully. "If I am not mistaken, no one here remembers how they, in fact, came upon this world."

Nina and Ruby shrugged and shook their heads "No," before Lily timidly raised her hand and spoke up.

"I actually do. I, um…" She suddenly seemed bothered by something, and began to fidget in her seat. "I kind of came back with him. We met after he had an…accident, and I decided to stay here after bringing him back."

For a while, no one spoke. It struck me as odd that everyone appeared to be so shocked – from what I had gathered, spirits and humans interacting was uncommon, but by no means unexpected.

"Did she do something wrong?" I asked, placing a hand on Lily's lap. I quite literally owed her my life, so it made me a bit frustrated to see her put in such an uncomfortable position over what she did.

"You see…" Athena started, but immediately trailed off.

"Are you saying she did something wrong?" I repeated, hoping that someone would give me a straight answer. I felt Lily's cool hand cover mine, as she looked at me shyly.

"Spirits aren't…really…supposed to do what I did," she said quietly.

"But I thought you came to this world all the time? I mean, it couldn't be that bad right?"

Once more I was greeted with an uneasy silence.

"The common lineage between spirits and mortals is… nuanced," Athena explained. "Though it is certain that the two kinds have been in contact near since their conception, it was always to be done under the strictest circumstances, and at that for only a temporary residence."

"So what you're saying is –?"

Lily nodded solemnly.

"When I came back with you, I gave up my ability to go back where I came from."

Even as I struggled to grasp the meaning of her words, a dull numbness emanated throughout my body.

"Why didn't you tell me? I wouldn't have asked you – I mean, I wouldn't have wanted you to give up everything just to –"

Lily looked up at me with a strained smile. "I did it because I wanted to be here with you. And…and…I didn't want you to worry about me. It was my decision to do this, and so I didn't want you to feel responsible."

Sighing, I clasped my hands around hers and shook my head. "You're a dummy, you know that? You don't have to keep these things to yourself – even if we've only been together for a short time, we share the same burdens."

Looking around the room at all of the other girls watching us, I nodded.

"That goes for everyone else here, too. I may not know what led us all together, but if you'll stick with me…I'll keep doing my best."

With a barely-contained smile, Athena shook her head. "You truly are a soul that never changes, I see. Still, I may be able to elaborate upon one of your inquiries, if you will allow."

"Please do."

"As I mentioned in passing, the connection between mortals and spirits – and, by extension, their respective worlds – is strong, yet unstable. The greater the number of spirits who enter the mortal realm – and abandon their stake in their original world – the thinner the separation between them becomes."

"So Lily coming here is what caused everyone else to show up, too?"

Athena nodded. "Correct." She paused and thought for a moment. "Or rather, I believe so. If a spirit was able to break the strongest plane set between life and death, then it is within reason that it cast ripples across the other worlds."

It seemed that again and again, just as soon as I was starting to understand these girls and where they came from, some new information came forward to throw me back into total darkness.

"Sorry everyone…" Lily whispered to the floor.

Maria shifted Nina in her lap and laughed softly. "Whether

intentional or not, I believe I speak for everyone when I say you have given us a wonderful gift in bringing us together."

"Agreed," Athena said politely.

"Mhm!" Nina, energetically.

"Yeph," came a muffled sound behind us – Luna must have had a rare moment of lucidity and spoke through the pillow she was still lying face-down on.

"Speak for yourselves," Ruby muttered, though a quick glance from Maria stifled any further protest.

"You see, without your choice to come here, I would have never reunited with my precious daughter, and none of us would have made the new friends we have here today."

Lily looked up and smiled at Maria, turning to me for confirmation.

"What can I say? I really do owe you everything – my life, the family we have here, the sense of happiness and purpose you all bring me. It sounds like you gave up everything just to be here, so...so I hope I can at least be a good partner."

Lily tightened her grip on my hand. "Still, I'm sorry again for causing everyone so much trouble. I hope you can forgive me..." She spoke faintly, still unsure of her own position in this whole mess of things.

Athena walked over and knelt down next to Lily so she could talk eye-to-eye with her.

"Nonsense, all of it. The whims of the heart overtake even the firmest of souls at times, and what you chose to do could be called nothing less of courageous." Turning to address the rest of us, Athena's voice took on a more serious tone. "If you will pardon the change in topic, I believe I can offer some further explanation."

I nodded, indicating we were ready to listen.

"I must stress that this serves only as a hypothesis, but I believe that the coincidences we have piled before us may be sifted out into a clear – yet however complex – pattern."

"So you're suggesting there's some connection to that pillar we found?" Maria mused airily.

"Yes, it seems a distinct possibility. That you, Luna, and even…er…I, myself arrived in this world near or around such structures seems beyond the realm of chance."

"Oh yeah, that's right – you never told us what happened right before you came here, did you?" I asked.

"I-it is nothing of much import," Athena said bashfully. Given it still appeared to be a sensitive topic, I decided not to press further.

"So…do you know exactly *what* would have caused us to come here?" To my surprise, the person who spoke up this time was Ruby. I had assumed she would've tuned out this whole conversation, but it seemed she was more engaged with what was going on than I initially thought.

"I must admit I do not. However, it is evident that the weakening of the planar divides – catalyzed, if not initiated, by Lily's crossing over – has only continued in this time. Though our only guide remains these enigmatic monuments, I believe we have made substantial progress in our novel investigation."

I raised my hand as Athena finished speaking, getting everyone's attention.

"Then I think I might know someone who can help."

29

knock knock

I lightly rapped against the pristine wooden door, perhaps afraid in my subconscious that any louder would disrupt the almost unnatural quiet overhanging the neighborhood. It wasn't unusual to see a small suburban area like this be somewhat empty on a work day, but given the timing it was as if each house was more a shell than a home – a grim facsimile of the real thing, yet lacking any of the trappings that would give it life. Still, I was certain this was the right address, so there wasn't much choice but to wait until Mae came to greet us.

"Are you sure she's home today?" Lily asked anxiously. It seemed even she felt a sense of unease in a place like this.

"Yeah, I checked with her just before leaving – she's probably tidying up or something, but still..."

I turned around to look over the small entourage that had accompanied me and Lily here.

"Are you sure it was a good idea to bring everyone along without telling her?"

"This concerns us more than you, human," Ruby said defiantly, narrowing her eyes at me.

Trying to shrug off what I had, by now, come to understand

was fully meant as an insult, I responded as placidly as possible.

"I get your point, but I still feel rude bringing over so many other people uninvited." I gave a dry laugh. "Knowing her though, this might be the greatest day of her life."

As if on cue, the door was pulled open without a sound and our small, excitable yet reserved friend peeked out.

"Hi Yuu, hi Lily, what's u–"

Mae stopped mid-sentence as she saw the five other girls standing behind us.

"Uh, hey Mae," I started sheepishly. "These are our friends. Do you mind if they come in too?"

Without a word, and as if in a daze, the petite girl nodded and stood to the side as our ragtag group of strangers-turned-friends-turned-family filed in one by one.

"I'm really sorry for bothering you on such short notice," I said as we wandered through the almost-labyrinthian style hallways that made up (at least what should've been) the majority of her home. Although the entryway was fairly unremarkable, the rest of the house seemed to be comprised of rooms and alcoves and nooks and hideaways branching off at every angle. It was by no means an ugly abode – it had that "lived in" feel, with just enough clutter to make it feel cozy – but the bizarre interior architecture was befuddling, to say the least.

"Oh, it's no trouble, really," Mae said cheerily, having gotten over her initial shock.

During the few weeks we had joined her for occult club activities, me and Lily had quickly come to find that Mae was never the most comfortable around new people. Part of me wondered if this accounted for the organization's dwindling membership, but I never had the heart to voice this suspicion out loud.

"My parents are usually away on some kind of business or another, so I almost always have the house to myself," Mae continued as we passed through what must have been the kitchen (given the strange layout, I had begun to forget what rooms we had and hadn't actually passed through). Still, there was no hint of bitterness or sadness in her voice as she spoke, which made me feel slightly self-conscious about the way I'd talked about my own parents in the past. I guess being on your own so often teaches you at least a little bit about how to care for yourself, in one way or another.

"Um, are we almost there yet?" Nina said shakily. "Nina's not feeling too good..."

Hearing this, everyone stopped and turned their attention back at Nina, who was looking significantly paler than usual. I looked to Maria for some kind of explanation, figuring she'd be the most likely to know what's wrong.

"Our kind have a very...keen sense of direction," she said carefully, maintaining an upbeat tone that sounded just a bit forced. "In cramped or sprawling corridors such as this, however, those senses can become overwhelmed. I believe that is all that's happening at the moment."

Maria gave a weak smile and ushered us forward, more concerned for her daughter's condition than her own.

"Alright then – "

Bending down next to her, I tucked one arm under Nina's legs and placed my other against her back, pulling her up and cradling her in my arms.

"I'll carry you like this the rest of the way, ok?" Normally Nina would protest when I scooped her up like this, but she must've been too dizzy to make much of a fuss, only offering a tiny nod in return.

"S-sorry, we're almost there," Mae mumbled as we continued to weave in and out of what I was beginning to think was an endless maze of hallways and offshoots.

"I don't mean to be rude, but is there any reason your house is built like...well...this?" I asked, starting to get a little light-headed myself.

"My parents are a little...eccentric," Mae explained slowly, trying to choose each word carefully. "I don't know the whole story, but the rumor I heard is that this weird man showed up in the area one day, rambling about an imminent disaster or something. I don't think anyone really took him seriously, but he kept handing out these really intricate drawings that kind of looked like houses, and, well – " She sighed in exasperation. "Apparently some people – my parents included – were inspired enough to use them as their floor plans. And now we have...this." She gestured in front a plain, white door, indicating that we had finally reached our destination.

"Didn't anyone think that was a little –"

I was going to finish saying "weird," but then remembered that I was in the company of spirits and nonhuman beings from other worlds, so a couple of oddly-designed houses seemed relatively tame in comparison.

"So, um, here we are..." Mae said as she opened the door and allowed us to step inside.

The room itself was of average size, making me further wonder how exactly so many other rooms were fit in what seemed to be a normal-sized house from the outside. From just a cursory glance, it seemed Mae was fairly particular when it came to organization – there was a simple brown desk next to two slim bookcases against one wall, and a small bed flanking the other, with not a single item eschew or, what I would guess, out of place.

"You really like to keep things neat, huh?" I wondered aloud as I took a seat on the floor.

"N-no, no, I just wanted to clean up a little before you came over is all." Mae's cheeks grew flush as she stammered out a response.

"An organized living space speaks to an organized mind," Athena said pleasantly, as she patted Mae on the head. "You should take pride in the work you have maintained here."

Catching Mae's curious and near-petrified stare, I couldn't help but laugh to myself.

"Sorry, sorry – I forgot to introduce you to everyone. You, uh, might wanna get comfortable though; it's kind of a long story."

Mae nodded and took a seat at the desk as the rest of settled in around the room. Despite the fact that we were packed into a single bedroom, the atmosphere was more cozy than cramped.

"So..." I began, trying to organize my thoughts. "You already know Lily and me, and I think you might remember meeting Athena and Nina before."

Mae nodded, taken in both rapt attention and wonder.

I gestured towards Luna, who was curled up in a ball on Athena's lap, the latter stroking her hair gently. "Also, this is Luna, another spirit. She, uh...doesn't really wake up much."

I now turned my attention to Maria and Ruby, who were still as much a mystery to me as they would be to Mae.

"And this is Nina's mom, Maria, and her friend, Ruby. They're both individuals from another world, but, um, not spirits." I struggled to remember how Ruby had referred to the three of them, but the specifics escaped me. Still, given her lack of retort, it seemed fair to assume that my cover was at least somewhat acceptable.

With the cursory introductions out of the way, I went on to explain everything we knew so far, and the situation we were stuck in. Though I couldn't say with any certainty, I was beginning to feel that it was more than coincidence drawing the girls, Whitehearst, and Rick together. The point that still hung over me, however, was even if I *did* find what was at the center of it all, would there be anything I could do about it?

"Hmm...I think I might've read something about that before. Give me a sec." Mae spoke up suddenly, snapping me back to reality.

With one motion, she pushed herself over to one of the bookcases, methodically looking over an assortment of volumes stacked together as tightly as the limited space would allow. From what I could tell, her hobbies at school were just as prominent at home – there was a seemingly endless variety of books on the occult, fairy tales, myths and legends, and something about "Real Magick for the Modern Age."

Their quality seemed...dubious, at best.

"Aha! Here it is –" Mae deftly pulled out a tattered brown book from one of the higher shelves and turned back to face us, an intense passion now ignited in her eyes. Even having spent a decent amount of time together in the club, the change in personality that overtook her when she was investigating otherworldly phenomena was as humorous as it was disquieting.

"Since no one was going to be around for the winter break, I decided to borrow this from the clubroom, just in case we needed it." With a bashful smile she looked up at me and Lily.

"I guess I was right. But anyway –!" Her lapse back into shyness was only momentary, as her fervor was once again front and center. "Let's see, let's see…orchid – no, ogre – no, omatia – no…"

Listening to Mae mumble on to herself, I only recognized about half of the words she was saying. Assuming this book was right about the other worlds, just what kind of stuff was still out there…?

"Finally! Obelisk!" Beaming with pride, Mae held open the book and propped it up on her lap for all of us to see.

"That's, uh, certainly something," I said, unsure as to what exactly I was supposed to be taking away. On the page was a hastily-scrawled image of a large pillar, though, compared to some of the other illustrations I saw Mae flip through, this one was oddly unrefined, as if the person drawing it was in a rush.

Lily nudged me, gesturing toward the page. "That's just like the one we found Luna at, remember?"

Thinking back on it, I guess there was some resemblance, but the illustration's choppy style coupled with the worn-down state we found the other pillar in made it difficult to call it an exact match.

I glanced at Maria, who was resting her chin on her hands and studying the page intently. After a few more moments of deliberation, she nodded.

"Yes, I believe that's the same type of object me and Ruby stumbled upon before arriving here."

"So…what is it, exactly?" I asked, still clueless to what this all actually meant.

"Well, according to this…" Mae said, running her finger over each line of text carefully. "These were ancient structures that allowed for a sort of link between the different worlds. They're supposed to be kinda like radio towers, in a way – it says here it's just a theory, but apparently in the presence of enough energy, they could activate and send nearby people –" Mae looked up at us and paused. "Or, um, not-people too, I guess, to other worlds."

I could see Ruby shift uncomfortably out of the corner of my eye.

"Why would someone make something like that, though?" Lily asked.

"Indeed, the defensive ramifications of opening not only one's borders, but the very fabric of their world to invaders are precarious at best…" Athena added, nodding sagely.

"So I guess you haven't heard of things like this before, either?" I asked.

Athena shook her head. "I will freely admit that despite my utmost effort, there is much I still sorely lack knowledge of. I apologize for my lack of assistance in this matter."

I patted her on the shoulder. "No need to be so hard on yourself. I just figured you're the only other one who might've already read about this kinda thing."

"Stupid human…" I heard Ruby mutter.

I looked back at her, puzzled.

"Did I say something wrong?"

She rolled her eyes and sighed. "The others might forgive your ignorance, but at the very least you shouldn't make claims you can't back up."

Still baffled as to what was bothering her so much, I looked to Nina for some help, but she only offered a shrug.

"I…know about it too," Ruby said at last, as if she was struggling to fight out each word individually.

"You do?" Lily asked, shocked.

"It's probably not even that helpful..." Ruby muttered.

"Wow Ruby, you're even more amazing than Nina could ever imagine!" Nina cut in, fawning over her friend's professed knowledge – if I didn't know any better, I almost would've thought it was a clever ploy to play to her ego and get her to open up.

"Eheheh, well y'know I learned a couple of things here and there..."

"So...what *do* you know about them?" I asked carefully, earning myself yet another scornful look.

"Normally I would never think to share this kind of thing with humans, but..." She looked to her side fondly, where Nina was listening with rapt attention. "Since Nina asked, I really have no other choice." Ruby then closed her eyes and took a deep breath. "My ancestors were the ones to build those obelisks. At least – that's the story I was told ever since I was a hatchling. I always thought they were just bedtime stories for the little ones, all about these other worlds full of things they'd never seen."

It dawned on me that my world here must seem just as fantastical as their worlds were to me. For as mundane as my life could feel, I guess it was still brand-new and exciting for people who had never experienced something like that before.

"Since I always thought they were just fables, I never really looked into it when I had the chance. I heard of a few in my clan – the older ones – who were insistent that we find them again and keep them safe. I guess it's a little late for that now, though..." Ruby uttered this last line with grim humor.

"Then...what happened?" Nina asked.

"I don't know, really. Some of them might still be out there, somewhere. But I'm not holding out hope – it's been long enough that any kin who did make it out are probably dead."

Without my noticing, Maria had leaned in next to me, whispering. "I don't know the full story, but from what she told me once, it's been at least a full millennia since her clan went missing."

I couldn't help but be dumb-struck by this addition. The fact that Ruby seemed so childish, despite being over one thousand years old, was a difficult fact to digest. Though with how she was talking now, I guess maybe there was more going on beneath her petulant veneer than I first assumed.

As if reading my mind, Maria nodded and smiled obscurely. "Dragons live a very long time, especially when compared to a human's lifespan. So please be patient with her – despite how she may act at times, she means well."

I gave a solemn nod as Ruby let out a small sigh. "Anyway, I'm getting off topic. You all wanted to know about those dumb relics or whatever, right?"

We offered our silent assent, waiting for her to continue.

"I really don't know much more than what I already told you. Just some half-remembered stories parents told their children a long, long time ago. Even if I could remember, I doubt it'd be of any use." A dark shadow passed across Ruby's face, more frightening than any forward threats she'd made yet.

Athena leaned forward, an unusually desperate look in her eyes. "I must ask that you try yet. Even an incomplete memory may yet hold the key to our rapidly entangling futures."

Ruby looked around at us, befuddled.

"Uh, she's just asking you to tell us if you remember anything more, even if you're not sure," I clarified.

Again, Ruby shook her head. "I don't remember anything

specific, except…except every story seemed to involve some kind of monsters or whatever. The elders always told the little ones to stay away from those pillars, but that was probably just to keep them from wandering off."

To one side I heard Mae mumbling to herself as she scribbled frantically on a notepad she had placed over the book. "Pillar… relic…monsters…dragons…"

"Something you wish to share with the rest of us?" Maria asked.

Mae's head shot straight up as she blinked several times – seemed she had lost herself in her own thoughts once again.

"Oh, um, i-it's nothing, just some silly ideas I was writing down…"

Maria didn't say anything in response, but only tilted her head to the side, her smile never wavering.

…

After what was beginning to feel like an uncomfortably long period of silence, Mae spoke up again. "W-well if you all want to hear, I don't mind sharing, even though I'm not sure what it means myself…"

"Anything you can offer is certain to be useful – thank you." Maria maintained a sense of calm composure no matter the topic, as if she expected any and every response she received. I was quickly coming to find this ability quite off-putting.

Mae took a deep breath, her hand quivering slightly as she held it against her chest. Had I not known better, I might've assumed she was just gathering her courage, but given past events, it seemed just as likely she was trying to maintain some amount of composure while talking about all this.

"While she was talking –" Mae nodded toward Ruby. "Something seemed strange to me. None of you remember how exactly you came here, right?"

Each girl shook her head in turn, glancing around at the others for confirmation.

"Given that we don't know much more, it seems the most plausible reason you – and any other beings – came here is because of these obelisks. But!" Mae held up one finger for emphasis, starting to really get into the role. "Everything I've read on magical items has suggested that they require a certain amount of energy to operate. For something to not only be powerful enough to transport beings across worlds, but also do so without the individual knowing, would require an immense source of energy."

"But don't spirits visit other worlds all the time?" I asked, thinking back to Lily and Athena's own experiences. "I mean, some of them would even make contracts, right?"

Mae shook her head. "While it's true that spirits from different worlds are supposed to have different levels of ability to communicate with humans, there's nothing I've read to suggest that they actually come here themselves. Instead..." Mae tapped her head, trying to think of a way to explain it in a simplified way.

"It's sort of like a projection, if that makes sense. When humans and spirits come into contact, the humans can usually hear and, in really rare cases, even see the spirit themselves, but that spirit isn't actually there."

"What she says holds truth, barring any inaccuracies natural to mortals' understanding of the other worlds," Athena said slowly. "Though I was only called to task in this world but a number of times, this would be the first that I myself am actually present."

Lily tilted her head to the side, somewhat troubled. "I guess for me it's a little different, given the things I had to do and all…" she said, trailing off. "But I never really stayed here for long, either. Once I found my partner, we always departed soon after."

I think I began to see where Mae was going with this.

"So everyone being here right now–"

Mae nodded. "Is an exceptionally rare sight. Normally the barriers between worlds are strong enough to prevent anything like this happening. But…" Mae tapped her pencil against the side of her notebook a few times, lost in thought.

"But?" Lily asked after a brief pause.

"If what this book says is true, to achieve something on this scale the obelisks would need an enormous catalyst to energize them…"

"So the quandary that plagues us yet is how, and why I presume" Athena finished.

Mae nodded without looking up from her notes. "Normally with something like this, the people using it would know what they're doing. It'd be pretty hard for someone to accumulate enough power to transport themselves to another world without even knowing it…"

If what she was saying was true, there was almost no way Athena, or Luna, or even Ruby and Maria could have somehow triggered an obelisk by accident (if that was even really how they came here in the first place). The one person who didn't fit in all this was –

"Lily."

She quickly turned her attention towards me, surprised. "Hm, what is it Yuu?"

"You're the only one who remembers coming here, right?"

"I…I guess that's true," she said quietly.

"Can you tell us anything about how you actually came back here with me?"

It seemed obvious looking back on it, but I had never really asked Lily how she even brought me back to this world in the first place. I guess at the time "magic" made about as much sense as any deeper explanation would have.

"Mm, it's all a little fuzzy, even for me. I only remember the pathway outside the estate, which led to a kind of gate that all the spirits would use to go between there and the mortal world. I had never heard of someone bringing a soul with them before, but I suppose there's a first time for everything, eheheh..." Lily gave a small laugh, trying to cover up her growing embarrassment.

"It could be then..." Maria spoke casually, tracing circles in the air with her finger. "That maybe each world is more or less connected to one another? After all, it would make sense for mortals to exist close to the realm they must pass on through."

"Yeah, but –" The nascent embers of realization began to smolder. "But what if that's exactly it?"

I could feel everyone's gazes shift towards me, which put a bit more weight on what I was about to say. Still, I was pretty sure I was on the right track. I just had to keep pressing on with this line of thinking, wherever it might take me.

"What if everyone's here *not* because of some overwhelming power, but because the barrier...border...whatever between worlds are thinner? After all, if Lily was able to get here just by walking through a gate, isn't it possible that if the things stopping travel between worlds were weak enough, even a small amount of energy could accidentally transport spirits and creatures and monsters without them even realizing it?"

"That is certainly an interesting hypothesis," Athena said

thoughtfully. "Yet, should it prove true, it leaves us at an even greater loss – for what reason would these barriers be weakening?"

"Alright, you got me there," I admitted, somewhat defeated. "Any ideas, Mae?"

Mae let out a sigh and shook her head. "I haven't heard anything like that happening before – again, if that is what's really going on, this would be a complete first as far as anyone in this world would know."

"Wh..."

I just barely heard Ruby whisper something under her breath. At risk of another verbal assault, I decided to probe her a bit.

"Any ideas?"

"Whitehearst, that bastard!" Ruby exclaimed, before catching herself and covering her mouth.

"You think he's involved?" Maria asked in a hushed tone.

"You told me he was always trying to collect artifacts or whatever, showing them off to all his friends. If anyone would be stupid enough to cause something like this, it'd be him." Ruby now turned her attention towards me. "You, human."

"Yeah?"

"You've met him before, right? Whitehearst?"

"Only once in person, when we found Nina. Lily was there, too."

"What did he say to you at that time?"

"It was a while ago, but there was something about regretting my decision, and that we'd meet again. In hindsight he sounded more like a cheesy villain than anyone really that threatening."

"He always did have a flair for the dramatic," Maria said with a sardonic smile, shaking her head almost wistfully.

"See! See?" Ruby was getting more and more agitated as

she spoke, jumping to her feet now. "If he showed up in this world, he must have had a way to get here and go back. Even if I don't know how, it's clear it all comes back to him." Ruby's eyes glimmered deep-seated rage.

"Still, even if it is him, there's no way –"

I lost track of what Maria had begun to say as I felt my phone vibrating in my pocket. I quickly pulled it out to see an unfamiliar number was calling. As I ducked out of the room and into the hallway, I could faintly overhear the debate between Ruby and Maria continue.

"Hello? This is Yuu."

A slightly gruff, mostly tired, and now all-too familiar voice greeted me on the other end. "Hey, kid. It's time for me to call in that favor."

CPSIA information can be obtained
at www.ICGtesting.com
Printed in the USA
BVHW061008210321
603119BV00004B/687

9 780578 823652